Gemma looked at the sprig of green plastic with tiny white balls. 'It's mistletoe,' she said. Her breath was a huff. 'I'd almost forgotten, but it's Christmas Day now, isn't it?'

'It is indeed.' Andy turned his head to smile at her. 'Merry Christmas, Gemma.'

She held his gaze and Andy knew in that moment that he was going to see her again. Something had started tonight that he wouldn't be able to stop. Wouldn't want to stop. He raised the twig of mistletoe above their heads as the lift slowed.

He only meant to give her a peck on the cheek, but she moved her head as the doors opened and her lips brushed his.

For a heartbeat, she stood very still. As stunned as he was.

'Um...have a Merry Christmas, Andy,' she whispered. And then she was gone.

'Yes,' Andy told the silent corridor, before he pushed the button to go back to the floor he needed. 'You certainly will.'

MAYBE THIS CHRISTMAS...?

BY
ALISON ROBERTS

First published in Great Britain 2012
by Mills & Boon, an imprint of Harlequin (UK) Limited.
Large Print edition 2013
Harlequin (UK) Limited, Eton House,
18-24 Paradise Road, Richmond, Surrey TW9 1SR

© Alison Roberts 2012

ISBN: 978 0 263 23103 8

Printed and bound in Great Britain
by CPI Antony Rowe, Chippenham, Wiltshire

Alison Roberts lives in Christchurch, New Zealand, and has written over sixty Mills & Boon® Medical Romances™.

As a qualified paramedic, she has personal experience of the drama and emotion to be found in the world of medical professionals, and loves to weave stories with this rich background—especially when they can have a happy ending.

When Alison is not writing, you'll find her indulging her passion for dancing or spending time with her friends (including Molly the dog) and her daughter Becky, who has grown up to become a brilliant artist. She also loves to travel, hates housework and considers it a triumph when the flowers outnumber the weeds in her garden.

CHAPTER ONE

'HER name's Sophie Gillespie. She's six months old.'

A surprisingly heavy burden, but perhaps that was because Gemma hadn't thought to bring a pushchair and she'd been holding the baby on her hip for far too long already. The A and E department of the Queen Mary Infirmary in Manchester, England, was heaving and, because it was Christmas Eve, it all seemed rather surreal.

Reams of tired-looking tinsel had been strung in loops along the walls. A bunch of red and green balloons had been tied to the display screen, currently advertising the waiting time as being an hour and a half. And if they were this busy when it wasn't quite seven p.m., Gemma knew that the waiting time would only increase as new cases came in by ambulance and demanded the attention of the doctors and nurses on duty in the department.

'Look…this is an emergency.'

'Uh-huh?'

The middle-aged receptionist looked as if she'd seen it all. And she probably had. There was a group of very drunk teenage girls in naughty elf costumes singing and shouting loudly in a corner of the reception area. One of them was holding a bloodstained cloth to her face. Another was holding a vomit bag. A trio of equally drunk young men was watching the elves with appreciation and trying to outdo each other with wolf whistles. The expressions on the faces of the people between the groups were long-suffering. A woman sitting beside a small, crying boy looked to be at the end of her tether and she was glaring at Gemma, who appeared to be attempting to queue jump.

The receptionist peered over her glasses at Sophie, who wasn't helping. Thanks to the dose of paracetamol she'd given her as she'd left the house, the baby was looking a lot better than she had been. Her face was still flushed and her eyes over-bright but she wasn't crying with that frightening, high-pitched note any more. She was, in fact, smiling at the receptionist.

'She's running a temperature,' Gemma said. 'She's got a rash.'

'It's probably just a virus. Take a seat, please, ma'am. We'll get her seen as soon as possible.'

'What—in a couple of *hours*?'

Gemma could feel the heat radiating off the baby in her arms. She could feel the way Sophie was slumped listlessly against her body. The smile was fading and any moment now Sophie would start crying again. She took a deep breath.

'As soon as possible might be too late,' she snapped. 'She needs to be seen *now*. Please...' she added, trying to keep her voice from wavering. 'I just need to rule out the possibility that it's meningitis.'

'Rule out?' The receptionist peered over her glasses again, this time at Gemma. 'What are you, a doctor?'

'Yes, I am.' Gemma knew her tone lacked conviction. Could she still claim to be a doctor when it had been so long since she'd been anywhere near a patient?

'Not at this hospital you're not.'

Gemma closed her eyes for a heartbeat. 'I used to be.'

'And you're an expert in meningitis, then? What…you're going to tell me you're a paediatrician?'

Like the other woman waiting with a child, the receptionist clearly thought Gemma was trying to queue jump. And now there were people behind her, waiting to check in. One was a man in a dinner suit with a firm hold around the waist of a woman in an elegant black dress who had a halo of silver tinsel on her head.

'Can you hurry up?' the man said loudly. 'My wife needs help here.'

Sophie whimpered and Gemma knew she had to do something fast. Something she had sworn not to do. She took another deep breath and leaned closer to the hole in the bulletproof glass protecting the reception area.

'No, I'm not a paediatrician and I don't work at this hospital.' Her tone of voice was enough to encourage the receptionist to make eye contact. 'But my husband does.' At least, he did, as far as she knew. He could have moved on, though, couldn't he? In more ways than just where he worked. 'And he *is* a paediatrician,' she added, mentally crossing her fingers that this information would be enough to get her seen faster.

'Oh? What's his name, then?'

'Andrew Baxter.'

The woman behind her groaned and clutched her stomach. The man pushed past Gemma.

'For God's sake, I think my wife might be having a miscarriage.'

The receptionist's eyes had widened at Gemma's words. Now they widened even further as her gaze flicked to the next person in the queue and a look of alarm crossed her face. She leapt to her feet, signalling for assistance from other staff members. Moments later, the man and his wife were being ushered through the internal doors. The receptionist gave Gemma an apologetic glance.

'I won't be long. I'll get you seen next and… and I'll find out if your husband's on call.'

No. That was the last thing Gemma wanted.

Oh…Lord. What would Andy think if someone told him that his wife was in Reception? That she was holding a child that she thought might have meningitis?

He'd think it was his worst nightmare. The ghost of a Christmas past that he'd probably spent the last six years trying to forget.

Just like she had.

Dr Andrew Baxter was in his favourite place in the world. The large dayroom at the end of Queen Mary's paediatric ward.

He was admiring the enormous Christmas tree the staff had just finished decorating and he found himself smiling as he thought about the huge sack of gifts hiding in the sluice room that he would be in charge of distributing tomorrow when he was suitably dressed in his Santa costume.

It was hard to believe there had been a time when he hadn't been able to bring himself to come into this area of the ward. Especially at this particular time of year. When he'd been focused purely on the children who were too sick to enjoy this room with its bright decorations and abundance of toys.

Time really did heal, didn't it?

It couldn't wipe out the scars, of course. Andy knew there was a poignant ache behind his smile and he knew that he'd have to field a few significantly sympathetic glances from his colleagues tomorrow, but he could handle it now.

Enjoy it, even. And that was more than he'd ever hoped would be the case.

With it being after seven p.m., the dayroom would normally be empty as children were settled into bed for the night but here, just like in the outside world, Christmas Eve sparkled with a particular kind of magic that meant normal rules became rather flexible.

Four-year-old Ruth, who was recovering from a bone-marrow transplant to treat her leukaemia, was still at risk for infection but her dad, David, had carried her as far as the door so that she could see the tree. They were both wearing gowns and hats and had masks covering their faces but Andy saw the way David whispered in his daughter's ear and then pointed. He could see the way the child's eyes grew wide with wonder and then sense the urgency of the whisper back to her father.

Andy stepped closer.

'Hello, gorgeous.' He smiled at Ruth. 'Do you like our Christmas tree?'

A shy nod but then Ruth buried her face against her father's neck.

'Ruthie's worried that Father Christmas won't come to the hospital.'

'He *always* comes,' Andy said.

His confidence was absolute and why wouldn't it be? He'd been filling the role for years now and knew he could carry it off to perfection. Being tall and broad, it was easy to pad himself out with a couple of pillows so that his body shape was unrecognisable. The latest beard and moustache was a glue-on variety that couldn't be tugged off by a curious child and it was luxuriant enough to disguise him completely once the hat was in place.

Ruth's eyes appeared again and, after a brief glance at Andy, she whispered in her father's ear again. David grinned at Andy.

'She wants to know if he's going to bring her a present.'

'Sure is.' Andy nodded. There would be more than one that had Ruth's name on it. Every child on the ward had a parcel set aside for them from the pile of the donated gifts and parents were invited to put something special into Santa's sack as well. Not that Ruth would be able to join the throng that gathered around the tree for the ceremony but, if her latest test results were good, she should be able to watch from behind the windows and receive her gifts at a safer distance.

'Of course, he can't come to deliver the presents until all the girls and boys are asleep,'

Andy added, with a wink at David. 'Might be time for bed?'

Ruth looked at him properly this time. 'But… how does he know I'm in hos—in…hostible?'

Andy knew his face was solemn. 'He just does,' he said calmly. 'Santa's magic. *Christmas* is magic.'

He watched David carry Ruth back to her room, making a mental note to chase up the latest lab results on this patient later tonight. He might put in a quick call to her specialist consultant as well, to discuss what participation might be allowable tomorrow.

Andrew Baxter was a general paediatrician. He was the primary consultant for medical cases that were admitted to the ward and stayed involved if they were referred on to surgeons, but he was also involved in every other case that came through these doors in some way. The 'outside' world was pretty irrelevant these days. This was *his* world. His home.

It didn't matter if the young patients were admitted under an oncologist for cancer treatment or a specialist paediatric cardiologist for heart problems or an orthopaedic surgeon who was dealing with a traumatic injury. Andy was an automatic part of the team. He knew every child who was in here and some of them he knew extremely well because they got admitted more than once or stayed for a long time.

Like John Boy, who was still in the dayroom, circling the tree as he watched the fairy-lights sparkling. Eleven years old, John Boy had a progressive and debilitating syndrome that led to myriad physical challenges and his life expectancy was no more than fifteen to twenty years at best. If the cardiologists couldn't deal with the abnormalities that were causing a degree of heart failure this time, that life expectancy could be drastically reduced.

Of mixed race, with ultra-curly black hair and a wide, white smile, the lad had been fostered out since birth but had spent more of his life in hospital than out of it and he was a firm favourite on this ward. With his frail, twisted body now confined to a wheelchair, John Boy had lost none of his sense of humour and determination to cause mischief.

Right now, he was making some loud and rather disgusting noises, his head hanging almost between his knees. Andy moved swiftly.

'Hey, John Boy! What's going on?'

John Boy groaned impressively and waved his hand feebly. Andy looked down and stepped back hurriedly from the pile of vomit on the floor.

'Oh…*no*…'

A nurse, Carla, was climbing down the ladder she had used to fasten the huge star on the top of the tree.

'Oh *no*,' she echoed, but she was laughing. 'Not again, John Boy. That plastic vomit joke is getting old, you know?'

Andy nudged the offensive-looking puddle with his foot. Sure enough, the edge lifted cleanly. John Boy was laughing so hard he had to hold onto the side of his wheelchair to stop him falling out and the sound was so contagious everybody in the room was either laughing or smiling. The noise level was almost enough to drown out the sound of Andy's pager.

Still grinning, he walked to the wall phone and took the call. Within seconds his grin was only a memory and the frown on his face was enough to raise Carla's eyebrows. She straightened swiftly from picking up the plastic vomit. She dropped it in John Boy's lap, which caused a new paroxysm of mirth.

'What's up, Andy?'

But he couldn't tell her. He didn't want to tell anyone. It couldn't be true, surely? He kept his eyes focused on John Boy instead. On a patient. An anchor in his real world.

'His lips are getting blue,' he growled. 'Get him back to his room and get some oxygen on, would you, please, Carla?'

He knew they were both staring at him as he left the room. He knew that the tone of his voice had been enough to stop John Boy laughing as if a switch had been flicked off and he hated it that he'd been responsible for that.

But he hadn't been able to prevent that tone.

Not when he was struggling to hold back so many memories. Bad memories.

Oh…God… If this was really happening, why on earth did it have to happen *tonight* of all nights?

The emergency department was packed to the gills.

Andy entered through the internal double doors. Serious cases were filling the resuscitation bays. He could see an elderly man hooked up to monitors, sitting up and struggling to breathe even with the assistance of CPAP. Heart failure secondary to an infarction, probably. Ambulance officers were still hovering in the next bay where a trauma victim was being assessed. One of them was holding a cyclist's helmet, which was in two pieces. The next bay had staff intubating an unconscious man. A woman was standing in the corner of the bay, sobbing.

'I told him not to go up on the roof,' Andy heard her gasp. 'I didn't even *want* a stupid flashing reindeer.'

The cubicles were next and they were also full. One had a very well-dressed woman lying on the bed, a crooked tinsel halo still on her head.

'Can't you do something?' The man with her was glaring at the poor junior registrar. 'She's pregnant, for God's sake...'

So many people who were having their Christmas Eves ruined by illness or accident. This would have been a very depressing place to be except for the numerous staff members. Some of the nurses were wearing Santa hats or had flashing earrings. All of them, even the ones having to deal with life-threatening situations, were doing it with skill and patience and as much good cheer as was possible. Andy caught more than one smile of greeting. These people were his colleagues. The closest thing he had to family, in fact.

He smiled back and reached the central station to find a nurse he'd actually taken out once, a long time ago. Julia had made it very clear that she was disappointed it had never gone any further and she greeted him now with a very warm smile.

'Andy… Merry Christmas, almost.'

'You, too.' Julia's long blonde hair was tied back in a ponytail that had tinsel wound around the top. 'You guys look busy.'

'One of our biggest nights. Have you just come to visit?'

'No, I got paged. A baby…' Andy had to swallow rather hard. 'Query meningitis?'

Julia looked up at the glass board with the spaces for each cubicle had names and details that it was her job tonight to keep updated. 'Doesn't ring a bell…'

'Brought in by a woman called Gemma… Baxter.' The hesitation was momentary but significant. Would Gemma have gone back to her maiden name by now? She couldn't have got married again. Not when they'd never formalised a divorce. Julia didn't seem to notice the surname and Andy hurried on. 'Someone called Janice called it through.'

'Janice?' Julia looked puzzled. 'She's on Reception. In the waiting room.' Julia frowned. 'If she's got a query meningitis it should have come through as a priority. I hope she's not waiting for a bed or something. Let me go and check.'

'That's OK, I'll do that.' He could almost hear the wheels turning for Julia now. She was staring at him with an odd expression.

'Did you say her name was *Baxter*? Is she a relative?'

Was she? Did it still count if you were still legally married to someone even if they'd simply walked out of your life?

Andy had reached the external set of double doors that led into the waiting room. He spotted Gemma the instant he pushed through the doors. It didn't matter that the place was crowded and it should have been hard to find anybody—his gaze went unswervingly straight towards her as if it was some kind of magnetic force.

The impact was enough to stop him in his tracks for a moment.

His head was telling him that it didn't count.

Their marriage had been over a very long time ago and there was nothing there for him now.

His heart was telling him something very different.

This was the woman he had vowed to love, honour and cherish until they were parted by death. He'd meant every single word of those marriage vows.

For a moment, Andy could ignore everything that had happened since the day those vows had been spoken. He could forget about the way they'd been driven apart by forces too overwhelming for either of them to even begin to fight. He could forget that it had been years since he'd seen Gemma or heard the sound of her voice.

What he couldn't forget was what had drawn them together in the first place. That absolute surety that they were perfect for each other.

True soul mates.

For just that blink of time that pure feeling, one far too big to be enclosed by a tiny word like love, shone out of the dark corner of his heart that had been locked and abandoned for so long.

And…and that glow *hurt*, dammit.

* * *

Sophie was starting to grizzle again.

Gemma bounced her gently and started walking in a small circle, away from the queue waiting to see the receptionist. What was going on? She'd been told to wait but she'd expected to at least be shown through to a cubicle in the department. With the drama of the staff rushing to attend to the woman having a threatened miscarriage she seemed to have been forgotten.

Had they rung Andy? Was he on call or…even worse, had they rung him at home and made him feel obliged to come in on Christmas Eve and sort out a ghost from his past?

Oh…Lord. He probably had a new partner by now. He might even have his own kids. Except, if that was the case, why hadn't he contacted her to ask for a divorce? She'd had no contact at all. For four years. Ever since she'd packed that bag and—

'Gemma?'

The voice was angry. And it was male, but even

before Gemma whirled to face the speaker she knew it wasn't Andy.

'Simon! What are you doing here?'

Not only was it Simon, he had the children in tow. All of them. Seven-year-old Hazel, five-year-old Jamie and the twins, Chloe and Ben, who were three and a half.

'Go on,' she heard him snap. 'There she is.'

Hazel, bless her, was hanging onto a twin with each hand and hauling them forward. No easy task because they were clearly exhausted. What were they doing out of bed? They'd been asleep when Gemma had left the house and they were in their pyjamas and rubbing bleary eyes now, as though they hadn't woken up properly. Ben was clutching his favourite soft toy as if afraid someone was about to rip it out of his arms.

A sudden fear gripped Gemma. They were sick. With whatever Sophie had wrong with her.

But why was Simon here? OK, he'd arrived at the house a few minutes before the babysitter had been due and she'd had to rush off with Sophie but...but Hazel's bottom lip was wobbling and she was like another little mother to these children and *never* cried.

'Oh...hon come here.' Gemma balanced Sophie with one arm and held the other one out to gather Hazel and the twins close. 'It's all right...'

'No, it's not.' Simon had a hand on Jamie's shoulder, pushing the small boy towards her. 'Your babysitter decided not to show.'

'What? Oh, no...'

'She rang. Had a car accident or some such excuse.'

'Oh, my God! Is she all right?'

'She sounded fine.' Simon shook his head. 'Look, I'm sorry, Gemma but, you know...I had no idea what I was signing up for here.'

'No.' Of course he hadn't. This had been a blind date that an old friend had insisted on setting her up with. Just a glass of wine, she'd said. At your local. Just see if you like him. He's gorgeous. And rich. And *single.*

There was no denying that Simon was good looking. Blond, blue-eyed and extremely well dressed, too. And...smooth was the first thought that had come to mind when she'd let him into the house. But definitely not her type. He'd been horrified when she'd said she had to get Sophie to the hospital and could he please wait until the babysitter arrived.

And…

'How did you get them here?'

'I drove, of course. You practically live in the next county.'

Hardly. The house was rural, certainly, but on the very edge of the city, which made Queen Mary's the closest hospital, otherwise Gemma would have gone somewhere else.

'What about the car seats?'

'Ooh, look…' Jamie was pointing to the area of the waiting room set up to cater for children. 'There's toys.' He trotted off.

'He didn't use them,' Hazel said. 'I told him and he…' Her breath hitched. 'He told me to shut up.'

Gemma's jaw dropped. She stared at Simon, who simply shrugged.

'Look, I could've left them in the house. If Jane had told me anything more than that you were a cute, single chick who was desperate for a date, I wouldn't have come near you with a bargepole. I don't *do* kids.'

Chloe chose that moment to hold her arms up, asking to be cuddled. When it didn't happen instantly, she burst into tears. Sophie's grizzles turned into a full-blown wail. Ben sat down on the floor and buried his face against the well-worn fluff of his toy. Simon looked at them all for a second, shook his head in disbelief, turned on his heel and walked out.

Gemma had no idea what to do first. Hazel was pressed against her, her skinny little body shaking with repressed sobs. Gemma didn't need to look down. She knew that there would be tears streaming down Hazel's cheeks. Both Chloe and Sophie were howling and...Where on earth had Jamie got to?

Wildly, Gemma scanned the waiting room as she tried to tamp down the escalating tension from the sounds of miserable children all around her. The action came to a juddering halt, however, when her gaze collided with a person who'd been standing there watching the whole, horrible scene with Simon.

A man who had shaggy brown hair instead of groomed blond waves. Brown eyes, not blue. Who couldn't be considered well dressed with his crooked tie and shirtsleeves that were trying to come down from where they'd been rolled up. But her type?

Oh…yes. The archetype, in fact. Because this was Andy. The man she'd fallen in love with. The man she'd known would be the only one for her for the rest of her life. For just an instant, Gemma could forget that this was the man whose life she'd done her best to ruin because the first wave of emotion to hit her was one of…

Relief.

Thank *God*. No matter what happened in this next micro-chapter of her life, she could deal with it if she had Andy nearby.

Her touchstone.

The rock that had been missing from her life for so long. Yes, she'd learned to stand on her own two feet but the ground had never felt solid enough to trust. To put roots into.

The blessed relief that felt like a homecoming twisted almost instantly into something else, however. Fear?

He hadn't said her name but he looked as angry as Simon had been when he'd stormed into the waiting room of Queen Mary's.

Or...maybe it wasn't anger. She'd seen that kind of look before, during a fight. Partly anger but also pain. And bewilderment. The result of being attacked when you didn't know quite what it was about and why you deserved it in the first place.

Gemma didn't know what to say. Maybe Andy didn't either. He was looking at the baby in her arms.

'I'll take her,' he said. 'You bring the others and follow me.'

CHAPTER TWO

THANK heavens there was a sick baby to assess.

It was another blessing that Andy had had plenty of practice in using a professional mode to override personal pain. This might be the best test yet, mind you.

Gemma's baby?

She had found someone to take his place in her life and she'd had his *baby*? A baby he now had cradled in his own arms as he led the way from the waiting room into the business area of the emergency department. Gemma was a good few steps behind him. He hadn't waited quite long enough for her to scoop up the youngest girl and send the oldest one to fetch the boy called Jamie from the playpen.

Jamie?

Something was struggling to escape from the

part of his brain he was overriding but Andy didn't dare release the circuit breaker he'd had to slam on within seconds of walking into that waiting room.

That first glimpse of Gemma had hit him like an emotional sledgehammer. The power of that initial, soul-deep response had had the potential to destroy him utterly if he hadn't been able to shut it down fast. Fortunately, some automatic survival instinct had kicked in and extinguished that blinding glow. Shutting off his emotional response had left him with a lens focused on physical attributes and…astonishingly, it could have been yesterday that he'd last seen her.

OK, her hair was longer. Those luxuriant brown waves had barely touched her shoulders back then and they were in a loose plait that hung down to the middle of her back now. Same colour, though, and even in the artificial glare of the neon strip lighting in here it was alive with sparks of russet and deep gold. She'd filled out a little, too, but that only made her look more like the woman he'd fallen in love with instead of the pale shadow that had slipped out of his life four years ago.

How much worse was it going to be when he was close enough to see her eyes? Nobody else in the world had Gemma's eyes. They might share that glowing hazel shade but he'd never seen anyone with the unusual gold rims around the irises and the matching chips in their depths.

So far, by concentrating on the small people around her, Andy had managed to avoid more than a grazing glance. He was still avoiding direct eye contact as he walked briskly ahead of her.

He was getting close to the triage desk now and Julia was watching his approach. Or rather she was staring at the small train of followers he knew he had. Gemma must look like the old woman from the shoe, he thought grimly. So many children she didn't know what to do.

The irony would be unbearable if he let himself go there.

'Space?' he queried crisply. 'Query meningitis here.'

'Um…' Julia gave her head a tiny shake and turned it to glance over her shoulder at the board. 'Resus One's just been cleared…but—'

'Thanks.' Andy didn't give her time to say that it probably needed to be kept clear for a more urgent case. The privacy and space of one of the larger areas would be ideal to contain this unacceptably large group. It wasn't until he led them all into the space he realised that isolating himself from the hubbub of the cubicles would only intensify the undercurrents happening here but, by then, it was too late.

A nurse had just finished smoothing a clean sheet onto the bed. Andy laid the baby down gently. Her wails had diminished as he'd carried her here but the volume got turned up as he put her down and she was rubbing her eyes with small, tight fists. Was the light hurting her? Andy angled the lamp away.

'What's going on?' he asked. It was quite easy to ask the question without looking directly at Gemma. Right now she was just another parent of a sick child.

'Fever, irritability, refusing food.' Gemma's voice was strained. 'She vomited once and her cry sounded…' her voice wavered '…kind of high-pitched.'

Andy focused on the baby. He slid one hand behind her head. Lifting it gently, he was relieved to see her neck flex. If this was a case of meningitis, it was at an early stage but he could feel the heat from the skin beneath wisps of golden hair darkened by perspiration.

'Let's get her undressed,' he told the nurse. 'I'd like some baseline vital signs, too, thanks.'

Hard to assess a rate of breathing when a baby was this distressed, of course. And the bulging fontanelle could be the result of the effort of crying rather than anything more sinister. Andy straightened for a moment, frowning, as he tried to take in an overall impression.

It didn't help that there were so many other children in here. The small girl in Gemma's arms was still whimpering and the older boy was whining.

'But *why* can't I go and play with the toys?'

'Shh, Jamie.' The older girl gave him a shove. 'Sophie's *sick*. She might be going to *die*.'

Andy's eyebrows reversed direction and shot up. The matter-of-fact tone of the child was shocking. He heard Gemma gasp and it was impossible to prevent his gaze going straight to her face.

She was looking straight back at him.

He could see a mirror of his own shock at Sophie's statement. And see a flash of despair in Gemma's eyes.

And he could see something else. A plea? No, it was more like an entire library of unspoken words. Instant understanding and...trust that what was known wouldn't be used for harm.

And there was that glow again, dammit. Rays of intense light and warmth seeping out from the mental lid he'd slammed over the hole in his heart. Andy struggled to push the lid more firmly into place. To find something to screw it down with.

She's moved on, a small voice reminded Andy. *She's got children. Another man's children.*

It was Gemma who dragged her gaze clear.

'She's *not* going to die, Hazel.' But was there an edge of desperation in Gemma's voice?

'She's here so that we can look after her,' Andy added in his most reassuring adult-to-child tone. 'And make sure that she doesn't…' The stare he was receiving from Jamie was disconcerting. 'That nothing bad happens.'

The nurse was pulling Sophie's arms from the sleeves of a soft, hand-knitted cardigan. Sophie was not co-operating. She was flexing her arms tightly and kicking out with her feet. Nothing floppy about her, Andy thought. It was a good sign that she was so upset. It wouldn't be much fun for anybody if a lumbar puncture was needed to confirm the possibility of meningitis, though. He certainly wouldn't be doing a procedure like that with an audience of young children, especially when one of them was calmly expecting a catastrophe.

Hazel was giving him a stare as direct as Jamie's had been. She looked far older than her years and there was something familiar about that serious scrutiny. The penny finally dropped.

Hazel? Jamie? There was no way he could ignore the pull into the forbidden area now. Not that he was going to raise that lid, even a millimetre, but he could tread—carefully—around its perimeter. Andy directed a cautious glance at Gemma.

'These are your sister's children? Laura and Evan's kids?'

He didn't need to see her nodding. Of course they were. Four years was a long time in a child's life. The last time he'd seen Hazel she'd been a three-year-old. James had been a baby not much older than Sophie and…and Laura had been pregnant with twins, hadn't she?

The nurse had succeeded in undressing Sophie now, removing sheepskin bootees and peeling away the soft stretchy suit to leave her in just a singlet and nappy. Sophie was still protesting the procedure and she was starting to sound exhausted on top of being so unhappy. Gemma stepped closer. She tried to reach out a hand to touch the baby but the child she was holding wrapped her arms more tightly around her neck.

'No-o-o… Don't put me down, Aunty Gemma.'

Hazel was peering under the bed. 'You come out of there, Ben. Right *now*.'

'And Sophie?' Andy couldn't stem a wash of relief so strong it made his chest feel too tight to take a new breath. 'She's Laura's baby?'

'She was.' Gemma managed to secure her burden with one arm and touch Sophie's head with her other hand. She looked up at Andy. 'She's mine now. They all are.'

Andy said nothing. He knew his question was written all over his face.

'They were bringing Sophie home from the hospital,' Gemma said quietly. 'There was a head-on collision with a truck at the intersection where their lane joins the main road. A car came out of the lane without giving way and Evan swerved and that put them over the centre line. They… they both died at the scene.' She pressed her lips together hard and squeezed her eyes shut for a heartbeat.

'Oh, my God,' Andy breathed. Laura had been his sister-in-law. Bright and bubbly and so full of life. Gemma had been more than a big sister to her. She had been her mother as well. The news must have been unbelievably devastating. 'Gemma…I'm so sorry.'

Gemma opened her eyes again, avoiding his gaze. Because accepting sympathy might undo her in front of the children? Her voice was stronger. Artificially bright. 'Luckily the car seat saved Sophie from any injury.'

'And you were here in Manchester?' Andy still couldn't get his head around it. How long had she been here and why hadn't he known anything about it? It felt…wrong.

'No. I was in Sydney. Australia.'

Of course she had been. In the place she'd taken off to four years ago. The point on the globe where she could be as far as possible away from him. Andy could feel his own lips tightening. Could feel himself stepping back from that dangerous, personal ground.

'But you came back. To look after the kids.'

'Of course.'

Two tiny words that said *so* much. Andy knew exactly why Gemma had come back. But the simple statement prised open a completely separate can of worms at the same time. She could abandon her career and traverse the globe to care for children for her sister's sake?

She hadn't been able to do even half of that for him, had she?

There was anger trapped amongst the pain and grief in that no-go area. Plenty of it. Especially now that he had successfully extinguished that glow. He turned back to his patient.

'Let's get her singlet off as well. I want to check for any sign of a rash.'

Gemma wasn't sure who she felt the most sorry for.

Sophie? A tiny baby who was not only feeling sick but had to be frightened by the bright lights and strange environment and unfamiliar people pulling her clothes off and poking at her.

Hazel? A child who was disturbingly solemn

these days. It was scary the way she seemed to be braced for fate to wipe another member of her family from the face of the earth.

The twins, who were so tired they didn't know what to do with themselves?

Herself?

Oh, yes…it would be all too easy to make it about herself at this particular moment.

Not because she was half out of her mind with worry. Or that her arms were beginning to ache unbearably from holding the heavy weight of three-year-old Chloe who was slumped and almost asleep, with her head buried against Gemma's shoulder, but still making sad, whimpering sounds.

No. The real pain was coming from watching Andy. Seeing the changes that four years had etched into his face. The fine lines that had deepened around his eyes. The flecks of silver amongst the warm brown hair at his temples. The five-o'clock shadow that looked…coarser than she remembered.

Or maybe it wasn't the changes that were making her feel like this. Maybe it was the things that *hadn't* changed that were squeezing her heart until it ached harder than her arms.

That crease of genuine concern between his eyebrows. The confident but gentle movements of his hands as they touched the baby, seeking answers to so many questions. The way she could almost see his mind working with that absolute thoroughness and speed and intelligence she knew he possessed.

'She's got a bit of a rash on her trunk but that could be a heat rash from running a fever. This could be petechiae around her eyes, though.' Andy was bent over the baby, cupping her head reassuringly with one hand, using a single finger of his other hand to press an area close to her eyes, checking to see if the tiny spots would vanish with pressure. He glanced up at Gemma. 'Has she been vomiting at all?'

'Just the once. After a feed. She refused her bottle after that.'

Andy's nod was thoughtful. 'Could have been enough to push her venous pressure up and cause these.' But he was frowning. 'We'll have to keep an eye on them.'

He took his stethoscope out to listen to the tiny chest but paused for a moment when Sophie stretched out her hand. He gave her a finger to clutch. Gemma watched those tiny starfish fingers curl around Andy's finger and she could actually feel how warm and strong it must seem. Something curled inside her at the same time. The memory of what it was like to touch Andy? To feel his strength and his warmth and the steady, comforting beat of his heart?

It was so, so easy to remember how much she had loved this man.

How much she *still* loved him.

That's why you set him free, her mind whispered. *You have no claim on him any more. He wouldn't want you to have one.*

His voice was soft enough to bring a lump to her throat.

'It's all right, chicken,' he told Sophie. 'You'll get a proper cuddle soon, I promise.'

He might well give her that cuddle himself,

Gemma thought, and the fresh shaft of misery told her exactly who it was that she felt most sorry for here.

Andy.

No wonder she had felt that edge of anger when she'd told him she'd come rushing back from Australia to step into the terrible gap left by her sister's death.

Andy had been the one who'd wanted a big family. For Gemma it had come well down the list of any priorities. A list that had always been headed by her determination to achieve a stellar career.

The irony of what she was throwing in his face tonight was undeserved. Cruel, even.

Andy was the one with the stellar career now. The grapevine that existed in the medical world easily extended as far as Australia and she'd heard about his growing reputation as a leader in his field.

And her career?

Snuffed out. For the last six months and for as

far as she could see into the future, she would be a stay-at-home mum.

To a ridiculous number of children. The big family Andy had always wanted and she had refused to consider. In those days, she hadn't even wanted one child, had she?

Sophie's exhausted cries had settled into the occasional miserable hiccup as Andy completed his initial examination, which included peering into her ears with an otoscope.

'I don't think it's meningitis,' he told Gemma finally.

'Oh...thank God for that.' The tight knot in Gemma's stomach eased just a little, knowing that Sophie might not have to go through an invasive procedure like a lumbar puncture.

Andy could see the relief in Gemma's eyes but he couldn't smile at her. He knew she wasn't going to be happy with what he was about to say.

'I'm going to take some bloods.'

Sure enough, the fear was there again. Enough to show Andy that Gemma was totally committed to this family of orphans. Their welfare was *her* welfare.

'Her right eardrum is pretty inflamed,' he continued, 'and otitis media could well be enough to explain her symptoms but I'm concerned about that rash. We've had a local outbreak of measles recently and one or two of those children have had some unpleasant complications.'

Gemma was listening carefully. So was Hazel.

'Kirsty's got measles,' she said.

'Who's Kirsty?' Andy's voice was deceptively calm. 'A friend of yours?'

Hazel nodded. 'She comes to play at my house sometimes.'

Andy's glance held Gemma. 'Have the other children been vaccinated?'

'I…don't know, sorry.'

'We can find out. But not tonight, obviously.' Andy straightened. He could see the nurse preparing a tray for taking blood samples from Sophie but it wasn't something he wanted the other children to watch. He'd ask Gemma to take them all into the relatives' room for a few minutes.

She could take them all home. Even Sophie. He could issue instructions to keep them quarantined at home until the results came in and that way he'd be doing his duty in not risking the spread of a potentially dangerous illness. Gemma was more than capable of watching for any signs of deterioration in the baby's condition but…if he sent them home, would he see any of them again?

Did he want to?

Andy didn't know the answer to that so he wasn't willing to take the risk of losing what little control he had over the situation. And even the possibility of a potentially serious illness like measles made it perfectly justifiable to keep Sophie here until they were confident of the diagnosis.

To keep them all here, for that matter.

Quarantined, in fact.

'I'll be back in a minute,' he excused himself. 'I've got a phone call I need to make.'

Thirty minutes later, Gemma found herself in a single room at the end of the paediatric ward. Already containing two single beds and armchairs suitable for parents to crash in, the staff had squeezed in two extra cots and a bassinette.

'Just for a while,' Andy told her. 'Until we get the results back on those blood tests and we can rule out measles.'

Sophie was sound asleep in the bassinette with a dose of paracetamol and antibiotics on board. The twins were eyeing the cots dubiously. Jamie and Hazel were eyeing the hospital-issue pyjamas a nurse had provided.

'I want to go home,' Hazel whispered sadly.

'I know, hon, but we can't. Not yet.'

'But it's Christmas Eve.'

Gemma couldn't say anything. The true irony of this situation was pressing down on her. An unbearable weight that made it impossible to look directly at Andy.

She heard him clear his throat. An uncomfortable sound.

'Will you be all right getting the kids settled? I…have a patient in the PICU I really need to follow up on.'

'Of course. Thanks for all your help.'

'I'll come back later.'

Gemma said nothing. She couldn't because the lump in her throat was too huge.

It was Christmas Eve and Andy was going to the paediatric intensive care unit.

The place it had all begun, ten years ago.

CHAPTER THREE

Christmas: ten years ago

'IT'S a big ask, Gemma. I know that.'

The PICU consultant was dressed in a dinner suit, complete with a black velvet bow-tie. He was running late for a Christmas Eve function. Gemma already felt guilty for calling him in but she'd had no choice, had she? Her senior registrar and the consultant on duty were caught up dealing with a six-month-old baby in heart failure and a new admission with a severe asthma attack.

The deterioration in five-year-old Jessica's condition had been inevitable but the decision to withdraw treatment and end the child's suffering had certainly not been one a junior doctor could make.

'You don't have to do it immediately,' her consultant continued. 'Any time tonight is all right.

Wait until you've got the support you need. I'm sorry…but I really can't stay. This function is a huge deal for my daughter. She's leading in the carol choir doing a solo of "Once in Royal David's City" and if I don't make it my name will be mud and tomorrow's…'

'Christmas.' Gemma nodded. She managed a smile. 'Family time that shouldn't be spoiled if it can be helped.'

'You've got it.' The older man sighed. 'If there was any chance of improving the outcome by heroic measures right now I'd stay, of course. But we'd only be prolonging the inevitable.'

'I know.'

They'd all known that almost as soon as Jessica had been admitted. The battle against cancer had been going on for half the little girl's life and she'd seemed to be in remission but any infection in someone with a compromised immune system was potentially catastrophic.

Over the last few days they had been fighting multi-organ failure and the decision that had been made over the last hour had been much bigger than whether or not to begin dialysis to cope with her kidneys shutting down.

Gemma had to swallow the lump in her throat. 'I just don't understand why her mother won't come back in.'

'She's a foster-mother, Gemma,' he reminded her. 'She loves Jessica dearly but she's got six other children at home and…it's Christmas Eve. She was in here for most of the day and she's said her goodbyes. It's not as if Jessica's going to wake up. You'll take her off the life support and she'll just stop breathing. It probably won't take very long.' The consultant glanced at his watch as he reached for a pen. 'I'll write it up. As I said, I know it's a big ask. No one will blame you if you're not up for it but I know how much time you've spent with her since her admission and I thought…'

Gemma took a shaky inward breath. Yes, she'd spent a lot of time with Jessica. Too much, probably, especially before she'd been sedated and put on life support. Certainly enough time to have fallen in love with the child and, if the closest thing to a mother she had couldn't be here at the end then someone who loved her was surely next best.

'I can do it,' she whispered. 'But…not just yet.'

'Take all the time you need.' The consultant signed his name on the order and turned to leave. He paused to offer Gemma a sympathetic smile. 'You're one of the best junior doctors I've ever had the pleasure of working with,' he said, 'but this isn't a time for being brave and trying to cope on your own. Every person who works in here will understand how tough this is. Take your pick but find someone to lean on, OK?'

Gemma couldn't speak. She could only nod.

It was the way she was standing that caught his attention.

She looked as though she was gathering resolution to dive into a pool of icy water. Or knock on a door when she knew that somebody she really didn't want to see was going to answer the summons. What was going on in that closed room of the PICU? Andrew Baxter had to focus to tune back into what his registrar was saying.

'So we'll keep up the inotropic support overnight. Keep an eye on all the parameters, especially urine output. If it hasn't picked up by morning we'll be looking at some more invasive treatment for the heart failure.' The registrar yawned. 'Call me if anything changes but, in the meantime, I'm going to get my head down for a bit.' His smile was cheerful. 'You get to stay up and mind the shop. One of the perks of being the new kid on the block.'

'I don't mind.' Andy returned the smile, aware of the woman still standing as still as a statue outside that room. He hesitated only briefly after his companion left.

'Hey.' His greeting was quiet. 'Do you…um… need any help?'

She looked up at him and Andy was struck by two things. The first, and most obvious, was the level of distress in her eyes. The second was the eyes themselves. He'd never seen anything like them. Flecks of gold in the rich hazel depths and an extraordinary rim of the same gold around the edges of the irises. He couldn't help holding the eye contact for longer than he should with someone he'd never met but she didn't seem to mind. One side of her mouth curved upwards in a wry smile.

'Got a bit of courage to spare?'

Andy could feel himself standing a little bit taller. Feeling more confident than he knew he had a right to. 'You bet,' he said. 'How much would you like?'

'Buckets,' she said, a tiny wobble in her voice. 'Have you ever had to turn off someone's life support?'

Andy blew out a slow breath. 'Hardly. I'm a baby doctor. I started in the August intake and I've only just begun my second rotation.'

'Me, too.'

'And your team has left you to deal with this on your own?' Andy was horrified.

She shook her head. 'I get to choose a support person. My registrar is busy with the other consultant on the asthma case that came in a little while ago and the other registrar on duty is in with a baby. I think it's a cardiac case.'

Andy nodded. 'It is. I'm on a cardiology run. Six-month-old that's come in with heart failure. I'll probably be here all night, monitoring him. At the moment they're trying to decide whether to take him up to the cath lab for a procedure. I got sent out to check availability.'

'Sounds full on.'

'It won't be. If we're not going to the cath lab immediately I'll be floating around here pretty much for hours.' Andy tried to sound casual but her words were echoing in his head. She was allowed to choose a support person. The desire to *be* that person came from nowhere but it was disturbingly strong. It was emotional support she needed, not medical expertise, and surely he would understand how she would be feeling better than anyone else around here. They were both baby doctors and he knew how nervous he'd be in her position. How hard something like this would be.

Andy gave her an encouraging smile. 'I could be your support person.'

* * *

Gemma could feel her eyes widening.

She didn't even know this guy's name and he was being so...*nice.*

Genuine, too. He had dark brown eyes that radiated warmth. And understanding. Well, that made sense. He was at the same stage of his career as she was with hers and he'd never been in this position. Maybe, like her, he still hadn't even seen someone actually die. Gemma could be quite sure that anyone else here in the PICU had seen it before. It didn't mean that they wouldn't be able to support her but they might have forgotten just how scary it was that first time. Not knowing how it might hit you. How unprofessional you might end up looking...

Gemma didn't want to look unprofessional. Not in front of people who were more senior to herself and might judge her for it.

Kind eyes was smiling at her. 'Sorry—I haven't even introduced myself. Andrew Baxter. Andy...' He held out his hand.

Gemma automatically took the hand. It was

warm and big and gave hers a friendly squeeze rather than a formal shake. He let go almost immediately but she could still feel the warmth. And the strength.

'I'm Gemma,' she told him.

'Hello, Gemma.' Andy's smile faded and he looked suddenly sombre. 'Would you like me to check with my consultant about whether it's OK for me to hang out with you for a while?'

Gemma found herself nodding. 'I'll ask whether someone more senior has to be there. But there's no rush,' she added hurriedly. 'I wanted to just sit with Jessie for a bit first.'

He held her gaze for a moment, a question in his eyes. And then he nodded as though he approved of the plan.

'I'll come and find you,' he promised.

It was remarkably private in one of these areas of the PICU when the curtains were drawn over the big windows and the door was closed.

Remarkably quiet, too, with just the gentle hiss of the ventilator and muted beeping from the bank of monitoring equipment.

The nurse had given Gemma a concerned look before she'd left her alone in there with Jessica.

'Are you sure you don't want me to stay?'

Gemma shook her head and offered a faint smile. 'Thanks, but I need to do this in my own time,' she said. 'And…I think one of the other house officers is going to come and keep me company for a bit.'

The door opened quietly a few minutes later and then closed again. Andy moved with unusual grace for a big man as he positioned a chair and then sat down so that he was looking across the bed at Gemma.

Except he wasn't looking at Gemma. His gaze was fixed on Jessica's pale little face. He reached out and made her hand disappear beneath his.

'Hello, there, Jessie,' he whispered. 'I'm Andy. I'm Gemma's friend.'

Gemma liked that. She certainly needed a friend right now.

For several minutes they simply sat there in silence.

'Do you think she's aware of anything?' Gemma asked softly.

'I had a look at her chart on the way in,' Andy responded. 'She's well sedated so I'm sure she's not in any pain.'

'But nobody really knows, do they? Whether there's an awareness of…something.'

'Something like whether there's somebody there that cares about you?'

'Mmm.' Gemma took hold of Jessie's other hand as she looked up. Away from the harsh strip lighting of the main area of the PICU, Andy's face looked softer. His dark hair was just as tousled, the strong planes of his cheeks and jaw a little less craggy and his eyes were even warmer.

But what was really appealing was that he seemed to get what she was doing in here. Why it was important. His posture was also relaxed enough to suggest he wasn't going to put any pressure on her to hurry what had to be done.

'I saw she had a guardian listed as next of kin rather than family but…' Andy shook his head. 'I still don't understand why it's just us in here.'

'She's fostered,' Gemma told him. 'She was in foster-care even before she was diagnosed with a brain tumour over two years ago and she's had major medical issues ever since. There are very few foster-parents out there who would be prepared to cope with that.' She knew she was sounding a bit defensive but she knew how hard it could be.

'And the woman who's been doing it has a bunch of other kids who need her tonight. She's been in here half the day and...she couldn't face this.'

'But you can.' The statement was quiet and had a strong undercurrent of admiration.

Gemma's breath came out in a short huff. 'I don't know about that. It's...' For some strange reason she found herself on the verge of dumping her whole life history onto someone who was a stranger to her, which was pretty weird when she was such a fiercely private person. 'It's complicated.'

Andy said nothing for another minute or so.

Then he cleared his throat. 'So...where did you do your training?'

'Birmingham.' Gemma felt herself frowning. What on earth did this have to do with anything? Then she got it. Andy wanted to give her some time to get used to him. To trust him? Given that she'd learned not to trust people very early in life it was a strategy she could appreciate. Oddly, it felt redundant. How could she not instinctively trust someone who had such kind eyes?

Her abrupt response was still hanging in the air. Gemma cleared her throat. 'How 'bout you? Where did you train?'

'Cambridge.'

'Nice.'

Andy nodded. 'What made you choose Birmingham?'

'I lived there. With my younger sister.' Gemma paused for a heartbeat. Reminded herself that Andy was trying to build trust here and it couldn't hurt to help. 'She was still at school,' she added, 'and I didn't want to move her.'

Andy's eyebrows rose. 'There was just the two of you?'

It was Gemma's turn to nod. And then she took a deep breath. Maybe she needed to accelerate this 'getting to know you' phase because she really did need a friend here. Someone she could trust. Someone who knew they could trust her. Or maybe it had already been accelerated because of an instant connection that somehow disengaged all her normal protective mechanisms.

'We were foster-kids,' she told him quietly. 'I got guardianship of Laura as soon as I turned eighteen. She was thirteen then.'

She could feel the way his gaze was fixed on her even though she was keeping her head bowed, watching as she rubbed the back of Jessie's hand with her thumb.

'Wow… That's not something siblings often do for each other. Laura's very lucky to have you for a sister.'

'No. I'm the lucky one. Laura's an amazing person. One of those naturally happy people, you know? She can make everyone around her feel better just by being there.'

'You're both lucky, then,' Andy said. 'Me, I'm an only child. I dreamt of having a sibling. Lots of them, in fact. I couldn't think of anything better than having a really big family but it never happened.' He shrugged, as though excusing Gemma from feeling sorry for him. 'Guess it'll be up to me to change the next Baxter generation.'

'You want lots of kids?'

'At least half a dozen.' Andy grinned. 'What about you?'

Gemma shook her head sharply.

'You don't want kids?'

'Sure. One or two. But that's so far into the future it doesn't register yet.' She could feel her spine straighten a little. 'I haven't worked as hard as I have not to make sure I get my career exactly where I want it before I take time off to have a baby.'

'Going to be rich and famous, huh?'

'That's the plan.' Oh, help...that had sounded

shallow hadn't it? 'Secure, anyway,' Gemma added. 'And...respected, I guess.'

Andy nodded as though he understood where she was coming from. 'How old were you when you went into foster-care?'

'I was eight. Laura was only three. Luckily we got sent places together. Probably because I kicked up such a fuss if they made noises about separating us and also because I was prepared to take care of Laura myself.' She looked up then and offered a smile. 'I was quite likely to bite anybody that tried to take over.'

Andy grinned. 'I can believe that.' Then his face sobered again. He looked at Jessie and then back at Gemma. He didn't say anything but she knew he was joining the dots. She didn't need to spell out the complexities of why she felt a bond with this child and why it was important for her to be here with her at the end of her short life.

'You're quite something, aren't you?' he said finally.

A warm glow unfurled somewhere deep inside

Gemma but outwardly all she did was shrug. 'I wouldn't say that.'

'I would. You completed your medical degree. It was hard enough for me and I had family support and no responsibilities. I've still got a pretty impressive student debt.'

'Tell me about it.' But Gemma didn't want to go there. She'd shared more than enough of her difficult background. Any more and they'd need to bring in the violins and that was definitely not an atmosphere that was going to help get her into the right space for what had to come. The task she still wasn't quite ready for. Time to change the subject and get to know her new friend a little better. 'What made you choose to go into medicine?'

'I think I always wanted to be a doctor. My dad's a GP in Norwich.'

'Family tradition?'

Andy grinned. 'Familiar, anyway. I just grew up knowing that the only thing I wanted to be was a doctor. Maybe I was too lazy to think of anything else I wanted to be.' His gaze was interested. 'How 'bout you?'

'Laura had to have her appendix out when she was seven and the surgeon was the loveliest woman, who arranged permission for me to stay in the hospital with her for a couple of days. I fell in love with both the surgeon and the hospital. Plus, I had to choose a career that would enable me to always be able to take care of my sister.'

'So you're going into surgery for a speciality?'

Gemma smiled. 'Haven't thought about that too much yet. I'm concentrating on surviving the next couple of years.'

'Me, too. I figure that it could be a process of elimination. It's a good thing we get all these rotations. I'll cross off the ones that don't feel right along the way.' He looked at Jessie and sighed. 'Might have to cross off PICU. It's pretty intense, isn't it?'

'But awesome when the outcome is good. What's happening with that baby that came in under your team?'

'He's been off colour for a few days but his

mother brought him in because he was so breathless he couldn't finish his bottle. We started diuretics in ED but his blood gases showed metabolic acidosis.'

'Has he got a congenital abnormality?'

Andy shook his head. 'Echocardiography was normal. The likely scenario is an infection of some kind. Viral or bacterial.'

'Will he make it?'

Andy looked grim. 'About thirty per cent of kids that are like this die or require transplantation in the first year after the infection. His parents are distraught. It's their first baby.'

His empathy for those parents was transparent and Gemma felt a flash of sympathy. Maybe it was a hazard of the job for junior doctors that they became too emotionally involved with their cases. Andy wasn't only prepared to care about his own case, he was now in, boots and all, to Gemma's.

He not only had kind eyes, this man. He had a huge heart.

'They're not bad odds,' she offered. 'Worth fighting for, that's for sure.'

'Mmm. Speaking of which, I'd better go and check on things. Like his urine output.' Andy got to his feet. 'Will you be OK for a bit?'

Gemma nodded. 'I…might take her lines out.'

'But you won't do anything else? Until I get back?'

He looked so anxious. So concerned. For *her*.

Gemma felt something very big squeeze in her chest as she smiled at him. 'No. I won't do anything until you get back.'

By the time Andy got back to Jessica's room, he could see that things had changed. Gemma had taken off all the cardiac monitoring patches and the ECG machine was silent. The IV lines were out as well, including the central line that had been in place beneath a tiny collar bone. No blood pressure or heart rate or other vital signs were being recorded now. The screens on the monitors were blank, which accentuated the soft lighting. The only thing left to remove was the breathing tube. The only sound in the room was the gentle hiss of mechanically moving air.

Gemma had not only removed the invasive lines, she had covered the wounds with sticky dots and cleaned away any trace of blood.

'She hardly bled at all,' she told Andy. 'Her blood pressure must be really low.'

'Would you like me to remove the ET tube?'

He was watching Gemma's face carefully. He saw the fear in her eyes that was quickly shuttered by their lids. She had amazing eyelashes, a part of his brain registered. Thick and dark, like her hair, and he was sure she wasn't wearing any make-up. Right now, her lips were unnaturally pale. It was the tiny tremble in her lips that really undid Andy, though. He stepped closer and put his arm around her shoulders.

'Let's do it together.'

So they did. Gemma peeled away the tape securing the tube in place with as much care as if Jessica had been awake and feeling the unpleasant sensation. It was Andy who slipped the tube out and turned off the hiss of the ventilator.

For a long, long moment, they simply stood there. One of Gemma's hands was holding Jessie's. The other had somehow found its way into Andy's and he gripped it firmly.

They watched as the little girl struggled to take a breath on her own. Her face was still. Peaceful, even, but the small chest rose and fell slowly.

Andy could actually hear Gemma swallow. Her voice sounded thick. So quiet he had to lean closer to hear the words.

'How long do you think…?'

'I don't know.'

They watched for another breath. And another.

'Do you think…?' Gemma had to swallow again. Andy could see a tear trickling down the side of her nose. 'Do you think it would be OK to hold her?'

Andy felt dangerously close to tears himself. 'Of course it would.'

He guided Gemma to one of the comfortable chairs that were always in these rooms for exhausted parents. He gathered Jessica's limp body into his arms and gently transferred her into

Gemma's. She eased the little girl's head into the crook of her elbow and stroked away a few strands of hair.

'It's OK, hon,' she whispered. 'We're here. You're not alone.'

God…this was hard. Much harder than Andy had expected it to be. He had to look away and try to breathe past the painful lump in his throat.

He heard Gemma start to hum. Shakily at first, with no discernible tune, but then the sound grew stronger and he recognised it.

'The "Skye Boat Song",' he whispered.

Gemma looked up and her smile was poignant. 'It was Laura's favourite,' she said very softly. 'It always helped her get to sleep, no matter what was happening around us.'

The tight feeling in Andy's chest got bigger. What kind of childhood had Gemma had? She had an inner strength that shone through, despite the vulnerability he was witnessing in having to deal with this heart-breaking event.

She was, quite simply…astonishing.

Jessica's breathing pattern had changed. She

would take a deep breath and then several shallow ones and then there would be a pause before the next deep breath. Cheyne Stokes breathing, it was called. A sign that death was close.

Andy kept an eye on the clock in case Gemma didn't remember to record the time of death. He moved closer too, perching a hip on the arm of the chair so that he could put a hand on Gemma's shoulder and let her know that he was connected here.

He could look down. At a brave young woman holding a child as if she was hers. As if she was loved and would be mourned when she was gone.

Jessica was gone a short time later but neither of them moved for several minutes and they both had tears running freely.

It was hours later that Andy saw Gemma again. Waiting for a lift. The doors opened just as he got close so he got into the lift with her. He hadn't intended to but she'd looked wrecked the last time he'd seen her in the PICU and he had to make sure she was OK.

It was Gemma who spoke first as the doors of the lift closed.

'Thank you,' she said quietly. 'For...before. I couldn't have done that without you.'

'Yes, you could.' Andy was embarrassed by her gratitude. He looked down and nudged something with his foot. What was it? He stooped and picked it up.

'What's that?'

'A bit of rubbish.'

Gemma looked at the sprig of green plastic with tiny white balls. 'It's mistletoe,' she said. Her breath was a huff. 'I'd almost forgotten but it's Christmas Day now, isn't it?'

'It is indeed.' Andy turned his head to smile at her. 'Merry Christmas, Gemma.'

She held his gaze and Andy knew in that moment that he was going to see her again. That something had started tonight that he wouldn't be able to stop. Wouldn't want to stop. He raised the twig of mistletoe above their heads as the lift slowed.

He only meant to give her a peck on the cheek

but she moved her head as the doors opened and her lips brushed his.

For a heartbeat, she stood very still.

As stunned as he was?

'Um...Merry Christmas, Andy,' she whispered. 'See you around.' And then she was gone.

'Yes,' Andy told the silent corridor before he pushed the button to go back to the floor he needed. 'You certainly will.'

CHAPTER FOUR

THE children weren't at all happy about having to go to sleep in a strange room on Christmas Eve.

'No!' Ben shouted when Gemma tried to lift him into the cot. 'No, no, *n-o-o…*'

'Shh,' Gemma commanded. 'Don't wake Sophie up.' Or disturb any of the other sick children in this ward, she thought. It was a privilege to be keeping all these children together right now, she knew that. Of course she would have been allowed to stay with Sophie but if the others had been banned, she had nobody to step in and help out at such short notice and she would have had to leave the baby alone.

With her spirits sinking a little further, Gemma remembered she hadn't even texted the babysitter she had arranged for tonight to see if she was all right after her car accident.

Ben curled into a mutinous ball on the floor, having squirmed out of her arms. He also began crying. So did Chloe.

'I want Mummy,' she sobbed.

Even though the door to the room was firmly closed, Gemma could hear the faint wail of another miserable child somewhere. Set off by Ben and Chloe?

'Come on, guys,' she pleaded. 'It's not for long. Here...' She crouched on the floor and held out her arms. 'Cuddles?'

Chloe stuck out a quivering bottom lip. 'You're... not...Mummy.'

Oh...*God*...

Gemma felt like crying herself. She wasn't Mummy. She wasn't even a beloved aunty, was she? She'd fled from being involved in the lives of these children four years ago before the twins had even been born so she'd been no better than a complete stranger to them when she'd rushed back into their world six months ago.

It had seemed like she'd been making progress. The children had gradually got used to her and she'd done her best to make them feel loved and as secure as possible. But Chloe's whimpered words had taken her straight back to square one.

Or maybe not quite.

Hazel heaved a world-weary sigh that should only have been able to come from someone with several decades more life experience than a seven-year-old.

'Aunty Gemma is our mummy now, Chloe.'

Chloe eyed her older sister. Big, blue eyes swam with tears. She turned back to Gemma, sticking her thumb into her mouth. Thinking mode.

The nurses had provided a box of toys in the room and Jamie was sitting in the corner, doing a big-piece jigsaw puzzle of a squirrel. He looked up at Chloe.

'I love Aunty Gemma,' he said. 'She's a good mummy.'

The matter-of-fact words were sweet praise indeed. Gemma had to blink hard. The smile she gave Chloe was distinctly wobbly.

Chloe gave an enormous sniffle, pulled her thumb from her mouth with a popping sound and then held her arms wide to launch herself at Gemma.

Ben wanted in on the cuddle, of course, and Gemma suddenly had her arms overloaded with a warm tangle of chunky, three-year-old limbs and sweet-smelling, still baby-soft hair. She even got a sticky kiss from Chloe.

'Bed now?' Gemma suggested hopefully a minute or two later.

'Will you tell us a story?'

'Of course I will.'

But with Ben in one cot, Chloe shook her head firmly when Gemma went to lift her into the other cot.

'Want Ben,' she said. 'Same bed.'

'Hmm.' Gemma was dubious. 'It would be a bit of a squash, wouldn't it?'

But Ben, bless him, wriggled to one side. 'Lotsa room,' he declared. 'Digger's not big.'

'Digger' was Ben's favourite toy—a soft, brightly coloured bulldozer. Thank goodness it hadn't been left behind when Simon had brought the children in because Ben would never get to sleep without it. Chloe was the same about Raggy Doll.

Gemma's heart sank. Where *was* Raggy Doll?

Chloe didn't seem to have noticed yet that her cuddly was missing.

'I think sleeping with Ben is a great idea.' Gemma lifted Chloe into the cot. 'You can snuggle up like kittens in a basket.'

'I want a kitten,' Chloe said wistfully. 'Is Santa going to bring me one?'

'Maybe.' Gemma knew about the Christmas wish. She had a very cute, soft toy kitten wrapped and ready to go under the tree. Hopefully that would defer the longing for the real thing. 'Jamie? Can you find a story in the box, please? Then you could come and sit on my knee and listen too.'

Had the nurse deliberately put a story about Christmas in the box for the children? Gemma wasn't sure if it was going to be helpful to remind them about how much their own Christmas was being disrupted this year but the two older children listened with rapt attention to a tale of siblings who thought Christmas was boring until they both became involved in the magic of a pantomime performance. The twins were asleep by the time Gemma was halfway through the story and Jamie was struggling to keep his eyes open by the end.

'I want to go to a pantomime,' Hazel said as Gemma lifted Jamie into a bed. 'Mummy always said she'd take us. "Next year."'

'I'll take you,' Gemma promised, tucking Jamie in. 'Your mummy and I saw *Cinderella* when she was about your age. It was her favourite game for ages afterwards, playing pantomines.'

'I want to see *Jack and the Beanstalk*,' Jamie mumbled drowsily. 'Like in the story.'

And with that, he was asleep. Hazel, however, looked far from tired.

'When will you take us?' she demanded.

It was on the tip of Gemma's tongue to say 'Next year', which was only logical. It was far too late to arrange anything for this Christmas season. But then she looked into her niece's wide, blue eyes and she could see something that just shouldn't be there. An understanding that life did not necessarily deliver what you most wanted. That dreams weren't worth having because they were most likely not going to come true.

If she said 'Next year', Hazel would hear an echo of her mother's voice and maybe she would try and protect her heart from yet more pain by assuming it wasn't going to happen. Terrible accidents happened all the time, didn't they? 'Next year' her aunt might not be here any more.

'I think…' Gemma was speaking cautiously because she wasn't a hundred per cent sure '…that some pantomines go at least until the end of December. If we can find one that does and I can find someone to look after Sophie, I'll take you all.' She offered Hazel a hopeful smile. 'I'll go on the internet on my phone and see what I can find out.'

To Gemma's surprise, she discovered there was a lot of entertainment for children available in and around the city. Why had it not occurred to her to look into this before?

'*The Wind in the Willows* is on for another

couple of weeks,' she told Hazel. 'That would be fun.'

'Mmm.' Hazel had a fingertip against her teeth.

'Don't bite your nails, hon.'

She checked her phone again. 'Oh...*Jack and the Beanstalk* is on until the end of December. Shall I see if I can book some tickets?'

''Kay.'

'You're still biting.'

'Can't help it.'

Gemma sighed. The bad habit had only started in the last six months and it was always worse if Hazel was upset or worried about something. She closed her phone for the moment and went to give the little girl a hug.

'Sophie's going to be fine,' she told her. 'Try not to worry so much.'

'But it's not Sophie that I'm worried about.'

'What is it?'

Hazel kept her chin lowered. 'We're supposed to leave Santa a snack. We always put a glass of milk and a chocolate biscuit beside the fireplace. Sometimes he's not so hungry because all the boys and girls give him snacks but he always drinks some of the milk and takes a big bite out of the biccie.'

Hazel gave a huge sniff as she turned to stare at her little brother. Jamie was as soundly asleep as the twins but Hazel lowered her voice anyway.

'I know it's your mummy and daddy that give you most of the presents,' she whispered, 'but there's always a special one that they don't know about. It's wrapped in special paper and it doesn't have a label. *That's* the one that Santa brings.'

Another little piece broke off Gemma's heart as she thought of the family traditions Laura and Evan had been creating for their children. The kind that would get carried on for generations.

She hadn't known and it was too late to find different, special paper and leave those gifts without a label. Worse, she'd labelled more than one already as having been given by Father Christmas.

Oh…help…

'If he sees that we don't care enough to leave him something to eat and drink, he might think we don't even believe in him and he won't leave the special present,' Hazel continued sadly. 'And then it won't be really Christmas, will it?'

'Oh...hon...'

How could she fix this? Take a label off some of the gifts? Suggest that Santa had liked their Christmas paper enough to use it again on *his* special gifts?

But it was only a small part of the real problem here, wasn't it?

The bigger issue was that it wasn't going to be really Christmas because Christmas was all about family.

These children had been precious to their parents, who had created the best possible environment in which to raise them. It wasn't just the gorgeous, semi-rural property with the good school available nearby. It was more the loving environment. Parents that could weave positive family values and unique traditions into the upbringing of their children and celebrate them with joy on occasions like birthdays and Christmas.

That was what was missing from their lives

now. The absolute security of that love and the demonstration of it through little things like the details of what happened on Christmas Eve.

Gemma was at a loss but she had to try and make this better somehow.

'I love you,' she said, pulling Hazel into her arms for a cuddle. 'I'm not going anywhere. I will always be here for all of you and I will always love you.' She took a deep breath. 'Christmas *is* different this year and I'm really, really sorry about that, but it's still Christmas and we'll make it special because we love each other and we'll be together.' She tightened her hold into an extra squeeze and kissed the top of Hazel's head. 'We'll do it together, OK? Make it really special for everybody.'

Hazel wrapped her arms around Gemma's neck. 'You're nice, Aunty Gemma,' she whispered. 'I love you, too.'

For the second time that evening Gemma felt herself far too close to tears. Partly, it was from relief that she had managed to slot into the lives of her nieces and nephews and earn their trust.

Their love was a huge bonus.

Sophie was stirring as Gemma blinked back her tears. A whimper became a cry that threatened to wake the other children. Gemma hurried to lift her from the bassinette.

'I can hold her,' Hazel offered.

Gemma shook her head, bouncing the baby gently in her arms. 'It's late, sweetheart, and you need to try and get some rest, too.' Tension was rising at the same pace as Sophie's volume. Chloe stirred and whimpered in the cot.

Gemma thought quickly. 'I'll take Sophie for a bit of a walk and see if I can get a bottle heated for her. She's probably hungry by now.' She eyed Hazel anxiously. 'I won't be far away. Just out in the corridor.'

'I'll be OK.' Hazel nodded.

'Look…there's a button beside the bed, on the end of that cord thing. If you push that, a nurse will come. Why don't you curl up on the bed and try and go to sleep?'

''Kay.' Hazel came close enough to drop a kiss onto the back of her smallest sister's head.

'Shh…' she told the baby. 'It's OK. Aunty Gemma's looking after you. She's looking after all of us.'

Hazel's words echoed in Gemma's mind as she slipped out of the room and closed the door behind her. The ward corridor was dim but she could see the lighted area of the nurses' station and wondered if it would be acceptable to walk that far. Or were they being strictly quarantined until blood tests revealed whether Sophie might have a contagious disease like measles?

A smaller, bobbing light came towards her. The nurse was pointing the torch at the floor but raised it to illuminate Sophie's face.

'Problems?'

'The other children are asleep so I didn't want her to wake them. Sometimes walking up and down and singing is enough to get her to settle again but I think she might be hungry.'

'Might be a good time to change her nappy. We can take her temperature and check on what's happening with that rash, too. Then I can see about a bottle for you.'

'Thank you.' Gemma eyed the door of the private room they had been assigned. 'Are we still being quarantined? Do we need to do the nappy in there?'

The nurse also eyed the door. There were several children asleep in there and Sophie's cries stepped up a level in volume again. She shook her head.

'We can use the treatment room,' she said. 'It's not as though you're going to come anywhere near any other children at this time of night.'

She led the way. 'I'm Lisa Jones, by the way. Night shift nurse manager.'

'I'm Gemma Ba—' Gemma caught herself but Lisa smiled.

'Baxter, yes?' Even in the dim periphery of the torchlight Gemma could see the curiosity in Lisa's glance. 'None of us knew that Andy was still married.' Her smile widened. 'It explains why so many women got so disappointed by never getting past first base.'

For Gemma, it raised more questions rather than provided any kind of explanation. Had Andy

avoided having any kind of meaningful relationship with another woman?

Why?

And why on earth did it give her a frisson of…
what…*relief*?

'We've been separated for some time,' she informed Lisa, her voice tight enough to let the
nurse know that the topic of conversation was
not welcome. 'I've been working in Australia.'

The lights in the treatment room were overly
bright. Sophie's increasing distress made further
personal conversation impossible, which was fine
by Gemma. She'd had no intention of gossiping
about her personal life but Lisa had nodded at her
statement as though she knew already.

And why wouldn't she? The kind of tragedy
and its aftermath that she and Andy had been
through would have been hot news on any hospital grapevine. She had to assume everybody
knew virtually everything around here.

Was that the explanation for Andy's apparently
monastic existence in the last few years? Had he
simply been successful in keeping his private

life private? Or did he have the same problem she knew she would always face—of knowing that any relationship she might find could never adequately take the place of what was missing from her life? And, therefore, what was the point of even going there?

No. Sadly, Gemma was quite sure that wouldn't be what, if anything, was holding Andy back. She had been the one who had failed to live up to being a good partner in their marriage. It would be easy for Andy to find more than a replacement to fill that gap in his life. He would have no trouble finding a vastly improved model.

The casually uttered words of the nurse went round and round in the back of Gemma's mind as she watched Lisa remove Sophie's nappy and expertly assess her skin for any sign of a rash.

So *many* women?

So disappointed?

'Her skin's looking good,' Lisa declared. 'Let's get some fresh pants on her and take her temp.'

Sophie's temperature had come down a little.

'That's excellent,' Lisa told the baby. 'We'll

get you dressed again, give you a bit more paracetamol and then you can have some supper. Maybe that will stop you howling, yes?'

But Sophie stopped crying even before the formula was prepared and heated for her. She stopped when she'd been buttoned back into her stretchy suit and Gemma had picked her up for a cuddle. Rubbing her face in the dip beneath Gemma's collarbone, the ear-splitting shrieks subsided with remarkable speed, although she could still feel the tiny body in her arms jerking with deep, gulping breaths.

'Ohh…' Lisa smiled at them. 'Look at that. She just wanted her mummy.'

Gemma opened her mouth to deny the title and say she was only her aunt but then she closed it again.

She *was* Sophie's mummy now, wasn't she? She always would be. Maybe her bond with her, her sister's last child, would be the strongest because Sophie would have no memories of anyone else being there for her.

And at this moment the sweetness of being able

to comfort this tiny person was overwhelming. The best feeling in the world?

Holding the bottle as Sophie sucked on it was just as good. Something in the way she held eye contact with Gemma as she drank tugged on a very deep place in her heart. The tiny hand curled over her big finger on top of the bottle added another poignant beat every time it squeezed rhythmically. Like a kitten kneading its mother's stomach.

Another nurse came into the central station as Gemma sat there, feeding Sophie. Her face was creased with concern.

'Lisa? Ruth's awake and complaining of a tummyache. Should I give her something?'

'What's her temperature?'

'Normal. Everything seems fine...but...'

'I'll come and see her. Did you check on John Boy?'

'His sats are down. Jules is watching him and she put his oxygen flow up to six litres. He's awake, too, I'm afraid. He's not complaining of anything, as usual, but I think he might need some additional pain relief. Should we page Andy?'

'Give me a minute or two to double-check. We don't want to pull him away from the PICU unless we have to.'

'John Boy?' Gemma queried as Lisa draped a stethoscope around her neck and picked up a chart. 'Is that really his name?'

Lisa grinned. 'Maybe somebody was a fan of *The Waltons*, way back.' Her smile faded. 'Or maybe it was just because he was one of far too many children before he went into foster-care. He's a neat kid. Has some pretty serious heart failure to contend with at the moment.' She picked up another chart.

'And Ruthie's battling leukaemia. We need to keep a close eye on any symptoms in case it's infection or rejection after her bone-marrow transplant. I'll need to check them both and maybe drag Andy back from the PICU. Not that he'll mind,' she added. 'They're both favourites with him.' She paused by the door to glance back at Gemma. 'Will you be OK?'

Gemma nodded. The bottle was almost empty. 'I'll take Sophie back to the room. She'll probably be asleep again by the time I get there.'

She could hear the muted sounds of increased activity in the ward as she walked slowly back to the room. Maybe Lisa shouldn't have been giving her any details of her patients' histories but that kind of confidentiality was more relaxed on a paediatric ward and she was a doctor herself. She certainly couldn't accuse any of the people she'd met so far of being unprofessional. Young lives were at stake here and the staff were clearly dedicated.

Including Andy, obviously. Both these sick children were favourites? And he wouldn't mind a late-night call to pull him back to the ward?

Gemma's steps slowed to the point where she actually stopped and turned for a long look down the ward corridor. She could see doors that were open and hear the squeak of a trolley being moved.

Right at the end of the corridor she could see small flashes of red and green and blue. There must be a Christmas tree in the dayroom, she decided. Of course there would be. She might have been away from dealing with patients for a long time but she remembered the extra lengths medical staff went to in order to make a day like Christmas special for anyone unfortunate enough to be confined in a hospital. That kind of effort always reached its peak when children were involved.

Rapid footsteps sounded and Gemma saw a nurse hurrying into the nurses' station. She could hear the low buzz of an urgent conversation, which was probably summoning Andy back to the ward.

To his world, in fact.

And suddenly Gemma understood.

She looked down at the baby in her arms and remembered that feeling she'd had when she'd picked her up and Sophie had stopped crying.

She'd never understood how Andy could have chosen to go into paediatrics after what had happened. It had felt like he was rubbing salt into her wounds. Like he was telling the world it didn't matter and that he could move on.

But did he get that same kind of feeling from comforting these sick children? And their families? How much would it be magnified by being able to save their lives or at least improve them, instead of only offering the comfort of cleanliness and warmth and food?

She got it.

Finally. Too late, of course, but Gemma felt humbled by the knowledge.

She tiptoed back into the room to find that Hazel had fallen asleep as well. She and Sophie were the only ones awake now and Sophie's eyelids were showing no sign of drooping. She grinned up at Gemma, who found herself smiling back.

She began to walk between the door and window. Back and forth. Humming softly to the tune of a song she knew would only soothe the other children and was therefore very unlikely to wake them. A tune that was automatic enough to allow her thoughts to continue tumbling unchecked.

* * *

Dear Lord…was that the *'Skye Boat Song'* he could hear?

It stopped Andy in his tracks outside the room that Gemma and the children were in. The door was slightly ajar, which was how he could hear the sound. The curtains on the corridor side of the room had not been completely closed either, so Andy could see inside.

He couldn't stop for more than a few seconds because he was needed elsewhere. The nursing staff was worried about Ruth. And John Boy. Neither problem sounded serious but he needed to check to reassure himself as much as his colleagues.

A few seconds was enough to take in the picture, though. Hazel was asleep on one of the beds, curled up with a blanket carefully draped over her. Jamie was asleep on the other bed, flat on his back and looking angelic with his blond curls and an amused tilt to the corners of his mouth. An opened story book lay on the floor near his bed.

The twins were in the same cot, a tangle of limbs in fluffy pyjamas that made them look like puppies in a box. A brightly coloured toy had been pushed to one end and was threatening to fall through the bars.

And there was Gemma. Walking slowly back and forth with her head bent low enough for her cheek to be resting gently on the baby's head.

It was the picture of a mother caring for her children. Andy could imagine the lilt of her voice as she'd read them a story. See her drawing up the blanket to tuck it around Hazel. Soon she would probably rescue the falling toy and put it back beside Ben and maybe she would smooth strands of hair off his forehead and give him a kiss.

The tenderness of the picture made Andy's heart ache. The yearning sensation stayed with him as he moved on to deal with his young patients.

It was still with him a little while later when he'd checked both Ruth and John Boy and charted extra medications to help them both get a good night's sleep.

He could feel the pull back to that room at the end of the corridor and it was so strong it hurt.

Or maybe it was something else that was causing the pain.

Trying to get his head straight, Andy walked in the opposite direction from the room that held Gemma and all the Gillespie children in it. He found himself in the ward's dayroom, staring at the coloured flashes coming from the lights on the Christmas tree.

Christmas was such a part of his and Gemma's story, wasn't it?

That first Christmas, ten years ago, had been when he'd met the woman he'd known was going to be the love of his life.

What if someone had asked him, a few weeks later, what he saw for his future? OK, maybe it had been later than that that the dream had taken firm shape but the longing had always been there, hadn't it?

A variation on the picture he'd been caught by when he'd come back into the ward a short time ago.

A loving family with Gemma at its heart.

Oh…how he wanted to go back to that room. But he couldn't make his feet move. What if she was still singing to get Sophie back to sleep?

The song she had sung to her little sister so many years ago to help her sleep no matter what had been happening around them.

The song she had sung to a dying child who'd had nobody around to love them at the end.

The song she had sung to Max.

The lights on the Christmas tree seemed to intensify and grow spikes of colour that blurred until Andy could blink the extra moisture away.

Christmas…

Family…

Gemma…

…Heartache.

CHAPTER FIVE

Christmas: eight years ago

THE cafeteria on the first floor of Queen Mary's hospital was even more crowded and noisy than usual.

The vast room was still decorated with huge, rainbow-hued paper bells and chains thanks to the staff party that had been hosted in here last night. The festive spirit seemed to have lingered as well judging by the peals of laughter amongst the hubbub of conversation, clash of cutlery on china and pagers and mobile phones going off. The faint strains of a Christmas carol could be heard coming from a CD player near the cash register.

Gemma eyed the food selection dubiously. 'Have you got any sushi left?'

'Long gone. Sorry, love. You're a bit late for lunch.'

'Tell me about it.' Gemma heaved a sigh. 'I'll have some macaroni cheese, thanks.'

'Good choice.' The kitchen hand nodded. 'You need a bit of meat on your bones, you do.'

As she pushed her tray further along the counter, Gemma's smile had nothing to do with the gelatinous heap of hot food on her plate. She was happy because she knew that somewhere in this crowded space Andy was waiting for her. And, if the Christmas fairies were kind, they might get a whole thirty minutes of each other's company.

It should have been almost impossible to spot a single person quickly amongst the hordes but Gemma simply stood still near the till, holding her tray. She closed her eyes for a moment, listening to the sound of a choir singing 'Oh, Come, All Ye Faithful' from the CD player and then opened her eyes and let something she couldn't name direct her gaze.

'Joyful and triumphant...' the choir sang, and they were right because it had worked.

It always worked.

Andy broke off the conversation he was having with someone at an adjoining table and his gaze zeroed in to meet Gemma's. He waved and smiled and Gemma let out the breath she hadn't noticed she was holding.

How long would it last? she wondered as she got closer. It had been two years since she'd met Andy in the PICU that night. Over a year since they'd moved in together and yet her stomach still did that odd little flip when she saw him smile at her. A flip that sent waves of something rippling through her body. Something strong and safe that had become her touchstone in a world that was often exhausting and challenging and difficult. Something that was also thrilling because it reminded her of what the world was like when it was just the two of them and they had a whole night to be together. Something that was joyous, too, because it held a promise of how good the future might be.

'Good grief, what *is* that?'

'Macaroni cheese. Want some?' Gemma held

up a loaded fork and laughed as Andy's eyes widened in mock horror.

'I'm OK, thanks. Up to coffee already, see? I had a turkey roll. With stuffing and cranberry sauce. Probably leftovers from the supper last night but it was still great.'

'Didn't see any of them. Anyway...' Gemma wolfed the forkful. 'I'm starving and carb loading is a good idea because I'll need the energy to cope with the marathon that will probably be the rest of my shift.'

'How's it going in babyland?'

'Flat out. You'd think people would time getting pregnant a bit better, wouldn't you?' Gemma spoke around another forkful of cheesy pasta. 'Two Caesars, a forceps and a breech. And that was all by elevenses.'

'Well, I've had two heart attacks, an amputated finger, critical asthma and unexplained abdominal pain.'

Gemma grinned. 'You're looking surprisingly well, in that case. Good job on the finger, too. Can't see a scar, even.'

* * *

It was an old joke but Andy had no trouble smiling back. For a heartbeat the cacophony of sounds, the harsh lighting and even the competing smells of various foodstuffs faded away. He could even forget about that awful stuff Gemma was eating. His outward breath was a sigh of pure contentment.

He could lose himself in her eyes like this every time. Especially when she smiled. It made him feel…good.

Really good. As if he was in exactly the right place in his life. With exactly the right person.

'Still OK for tonight?' It wasn't beyond the realms of possibility that Gemma would have put her hand up for an extra shift if things were desperate.

'Can't wait.' Gemma ate another mouthful and chased a drop of cheese sauce from her lips with her tongue.

Andy's gut tightened pleasurably. He couldn't wait either.

'How good is it that we've both got Christmas Eve off duty?'

'I know. Sometimes I wonder why we bothered moving in together when we only see each other in here or when we bump into each other in some corridor.'

'Because we've both got horrendous student debts and two can live as cheaply as one.'

They both smiled. They both knew the real reason why they had moved in together and it wasn't simply to save money. It had been the logical next step in a relationship that had the potential to last for ever.

'Speaking of debt,' Andy said, 'I've checked online and the bank holidays mean we've got a few days' grace to pay the power bill. That means you've got a bit extra for the groceries.'

'Hooray.' Gemma's eyes lit up. 'Chocolate.'

'I was thinking maybe a bottle of wine? For tonight?'

'Mmm. Chocolate *and* wine. Heaven.'

'Maybe some food, too?'

'Hmm.' Still eating, Gemma pulled a notebook

and pen from her pocket. 'I'd better write a list. You're on a late day, aren't you?'

'Yeah…sorry. Won't finish till eight p.m. at the earliest. Supermarkets will be shut by then, otherwise I'd come and help you shop.'

Gemma shook her head. 'How often do we get an evening with neither of us rostered on? I don't want to waste it in the aisles of a supermarket.' She glanced at Andy as he drained his coffee cup. 'We're out of coffee at home, aren't we?'

'Yep. And milk and bread. And I used the last of the shampoo this morning.'

Gemma scribbled the items on the list. 'I'll get some bacon and eggs for Christmas breakfast. It's good that we're working tomorrow, isn't it? We should get a nice Christmas lunch and that'll save us buying our own turkey.'

'The perks of being a junior doctor,' Andy agreed wryly. 'Overworked and underpaid but… hey…we get a free Christmas lunch.'

'At least you don't have to dress up in a Santa suit. You should see the party they're organising in the paediatric ward.'

'I did. I went up to check on that kid that came into A and E last night. The one that got hit by the car that lost control on the ice?'

'Oh…how's she doing?'

'Fractured pelvis and ribs but it was the head injury I was really worried about. CT was clear. Just bad concussion.' Andy knew he was sounding pleased. It had been a full-on resuscitation that he'd run by himself. He *was* pleased with the outcome.

Gemma looked up from her expanding list. She smiled. 'You're loving Emergency, aren't you?'

'Who wouldn't? You get a bit of everything. Neonates to geriatrics. Superficial to critical. Medical, surgical and trauma. It's a roller-coaster.'

'You want to choose it for a specialty?'

'You know? I think I might.' The thought of taking another step into shaping the future into exactly what he wanted it to look like was a great feeling. It would be perfect if Gemma could find that kind of satisfaction as well. They were due to nominate the specialty they would become a registrar in for the coming year but Gemma was using her head rather than her heart to try and make the decisions that would shape the rest of her career.

She wanted something that would have a re-search component that could take that career to medical-rock-star level. So far, the real contend-ers were either oncology or anaesthetics with a sub-specialty of pain control.

'You're going to cross O&G off your list, aren't you?'

Gemma nodded emphatically. 'It's not for me. All those *babies*…'

She was pulling an overly dramatic face but her final word seemed to hang in the air and suddenly a charged silence fell between them. A kitchen hand pushed a trolley past their table. She gathered up Andy's plate and cup and stacked them. She eyed Gemma's unfinished plate.

'You all done with that?'

'What? Oh…yes. I've had enough.'

Clearly, Gemma had lost the voracious appetite she'd arrived with. They both watched her plate being scraped and stacked and the cutlery being dropped into a bucket of sudsy water. Then they looked at each other and Andy raised his eyebrows in a silent question.

Gemma shook her head and looked away again. Oh...*hell*...

He reached out to give Gemma's hand a reassuring squeeze. 'It's only been a couple of days, babe. You're on the Pill and the percentage failure rate is ridiculously small. Stop stressing.'

'One per cent isn't ridiculously small, you know. Not if it happens to be you.'

'Try to think of it as a ninety-nine per cent chance of there being nothing to worry about.'

The sound of pagers going off was just part of the background noise in the busy cafeteria full of medics but this time it was close enough to make them both reach for the devices clipped to their belts.

'It's me.' Gemma sighed. 'Probably another Caesar, the rate we're going today. Nobody wants to wait and have their baby on Christmas Day.'

'I'll come with you. I was due back downstairs about five minutes ago, I think.'

Saying nothing as they edged their way between tables was fine but the silence was noticeable as soon as they left the cafeteria. A short walk took them to the bank of lifts where they had to part company. Gemma had to wait for a lift while Andy took the stairs down to the ground level. It wasn't much of a wait. The light glowed and a pinging sound announced the arrival of the lift.

'See you tonight.' Gemma's smile was a bit tight and Andy could see the shadow of anxiety in her eyes.

To hell with hospital etiquette, he decided, bending his head to brush her lips with his own.

'Stop worrying,' he said softly. 'Doctor's orders.'

Stop worrying?

Fat chance. But it was possible to shove the worry into a parking lot at the back of her brain. It was something that junior doctors got very practised at. All that worry over the last couple of years…

Could they handle the responsibility of being *real* doctors with lives affected by their decisions?

Could they cope with the exhaustion of long hours and having every job that more senior staff couldn't be bothered doing thrown their way?

Could they even begin to make a dent in the massive amount of debt they'd accumulated in their training?

You had to be dedicated to a career in medicine, that was for sure. But that was part of what had drawn Gemma and Andy together in the first place. They might have come into medicine from different directions but the determination to excel in a career they were both in love with was something they shared. Maybe that was why the relationship worked so well even when it was hard to find any quality time together to nurture it. They both understood the pressures and made allowances for it. Most of the time, anyway.

Gemma filled her trolley at the supermarket rapidly but she was being careful of what she pulled from the shelves and freezers. Only the essentials and the least expensive options. Except she had leeway to be just a little bit extravagant today, didn't she? It was Christmas and although they'd made a pact not to spend anything on buying presents for each other, it would be a gift in itself to have a special evening together. A nice dinner by candlelight. Wine. An early night…

A smile tugged at Gemma's lips as she chose Andy's favourite red wine and then went to find some steak to go with it. Maybe it was partly due to the pressure and small amount of time they had together at home that meant their love-making had never lost the magic of that first time, only a few days after their first meeting. If anything, it had got better and better as they learned more about each other and had fallen in love and chosen to make a commitment.

That love was growing stronger as time went by as well. Just thinking about Andy as she manoeuvred the trolley through crowded aisles gave Gemma the kind of warm internal glow that only her little sister had ever evoked in her before. The kind that made you want to cherish and nurture someone. The kind of giving that actually meant you could receive more than you gave.

Passing a Christmas confectionery stand, Gemma added a couple of candy canes, a big bag of cheesy ring snacks and the ultimate treat of her favourite brand of Swiss chocolate that came in the shape of gold-wrapped reindeer with red ribbons and bells around their necks. Andy wouldn't be as excited about the chocolate as she was and, still feeling the glow, Gemma wanted to find something special just for him. She headed for the toiletries section with the intention of at least checking out the price of aftershave or something. They needed shampoo, anyway, didn't they?

She walked past the over-the-counter medications first and the slim, blue and white boxes on the bottom shelf seemed to be glowing. The price on the home pregnancy test kits was high but Gemma stopped in her tracks. She even picked a box up.

It would be the best Christmas gift for both of

them, wouldn't it? To find that they weren't in that unlucky one per cent? To know that the future was still wide open and full of promise?

After a long moment she reluctantly returned the box to the shelf. She could do a test for free at work and what possible difference could waiting a day or two make? What if the news was what she so desperately didn't want it to be and Christmas was ruined for both of them? Gemma turned and fled the aisle, any thoughts of after-shave or even shampoo forgotten.

Her mobile was ringing as she headed out into the freezing, dark evening, laden with shopping bags. She had to put down two of the bags to reach her phone but she couldn't ignore the call. What if it was Andy, saying he was going to have to work later than expected? It would be an awful waste if she'd spent so much on a special dinner and then it was ruined by having to be kept warm for too long.

But it wasn't Andy.

'Laura!' Gemma forgot about how cold it was,

standing out here. 'Hey, hon...how *are* you? Merry almost Christmas. Did you get my card?'

Her little sister was laughing. 'Good and yes and same to you...'

'Did you get some time off work? Are you going to be able to come up?'

'Yes, but—'

'Oh...' Gemma couldn't help interrupting. 'It'll be so good to see you. It's been way too long.'

'I know. Gem?'

Gemma caught her breath. 'What?'

'I've got something to tell you.'

Gemma was still holding that breath. 'Oh, my God, you're not pregnant, are you?'

'*No...*' Laura was laughing again. 'At least, not yet.'

'What does that mean? You're *planning* to be pregnant?' Gemma had to shake her head. This was more than ironic.

'Ev's asked me to marry him, Gem. We're *engaged*. I've got a ring and everything.'

'Oh...' Gemma was lost for words. Laura sounded *so* happy. She was only twenty-two but her boyfriend Evan had been in her life for longer than Andy had been in hers. A builder with a solid future ahead of him, Evan had met Laura when he'd gone into the kitchen shop she worked in. 'That's fantastic, hon. I'm so happy for you.'

'That's not even the best bit. You know how Evan's always had a dream of finding some ramshackle old barn and converting it into a dream house? Well, he's found one on the internet and... you'll never guess.'

Gemma's heart skipped a beat. 'Don't tell me it's in Australia or somewhere.'

'No, silly. It's in spitting distance of you. Outskirts of Manchester. We've put an offer in. We should know whether we've got it or not by the time we come up to see you for New Year...' Laura's excitement was almost palpable. 'I can't wait... Will you help me plan my wedding?'

'Of course I will.'

'It'll be your turn next. We can make an extra scrapbook of ideas for you.'

It was Gemma's turn to laugh. 'As if... It'll be ten years before I've got time to even think about a wedding.' After all, why would you go to the expense of having a wedding unless you were ready to settle down and start a family?

'And keep your fingers crossed for us about the barn. How good would it be if we got it? There's even room for a pony for the kids. Hey…is it snowing up your way?'

Gemma looked around. The freezing sleet had, indeed, turned to fluffy white flakes while she'd been standing here, talking. 'Sure is, and I'm freezing. I need to get my groceries home and get some dinner on. Love you. I'll call you tomorrow.'

'Love you, too. Say hi to Andy for me.'

The snow was beginning to settle as Gemma reached the iron railing that marked her destination. She glanced below street level at the two-metre square of concrete that was the garden their basement bedsit looked out on.

A converted semi-rural barn? Settling down to make babies and even planning ahead for the pets those children would have?

Did she feel envious of her little sister?

Maybe a little but only because Laura was achieving her dream. They wanted very different things from life and Gemma still had a mountain to climb before she reached hers. There was a touch of sadness there too, letting go of the responsibility she'd had since childhood of protecting the person she loved most in the world. She could turn over that responsibility to Evan now, with the absolute confidence that he would step up to the mark.

Mixed in with both those realisations was also a definite fizzle of excitement. Background parental-type anxiety about Laura had always been there and had sometimes distracted her from her own goals.

That distraction was gone. She could focus on climbing her personal mountain now and eventually, like Laura, she would achieve everything she'd always dreamed of.

Andy spotted the tree branch beside a rubbish skip near the bus stop.

It must have broken off a good-sized Christmas tree a few days ago, he decided, because it was a bit wilted and had a ragged strip of bark at its base. Still…it was a good three feet high and not that lopsided. If he held it at an angle it looked like a small Christmas tree.

Just the right size for a very small apartment.

His feet crunched in a thin layer of snow when he got off the bus. A white Christmas this year, then. The best kind. Even a thin layer smoothed out the rough edges and made everything look a bit softer and prettier. The bare concrete yard beside the steps down to his front door looked positively festive with the glow of light coming through the gap where the curtain was frayed.

The smell of hot food as he went inside was mouth-watering. Gemma's face when she saw what he was carrying was priceless.

'For me? You shouldn't have…' She was laughing as Andy propped the branch against the end of the couch and swept her into a hug.

'Nothing's too much trouble for the woman I love,' he said. 'I had to put up with several people who didn't want to be close to a prickly pine tree on the bus but I just said, "Merry Christmas to you, too". And I smiled a lot.'

Gemma was smiling now. Right into his eyes. And then she gave him a kiss that was a promise of things to come. 'It's gorgeous,' she told him. 'And I know just what we can use to decorate it.'

They propped the branch up with medical text-books from their bookshelf. Gemma ripped open the bag of cheesy rings and held one up. 'Per-fect, yes?'

'Mmm.' Andy snatched the ring and ate it.

'No-o-o...' Gemma held the bag out of reach. 'Look.' She took a ring out and poked the end of a branch through its centre. The lurid yellow coating of the snack food stood out against the dark green of the pine needles.

By the time the bag was empty their fingers had a thick yellow coating as well but the small tree looked as though it was covered with oddly shaped golden lights. Gemma put her head on one side as she considered the final result. Grinning, she went to fetch something from a grocery bag beside the kitchen bench.

Using a knife, she poked a hole into the bottom of the gold-wrapped chocolate reindeer and then poked the uppermost point of the tree inside. The heavy ornament tipped sideways at a drunken angle but it didn't fall off. Gemma nodded with satisfaction.

'Perfect,' she declared. 'All it needs now is a pile of gifts underneath.' She caught her bottom lip between her teeth, turning to Andy. 'I haven't got a gift for you, babe, I'm sorry.'

'We made a pact, remember? But…I do have a gift for you…kind of.'

Gemma thumped his shoulder. 'How could you? What about the pact? Now I feel *really* awful.'

'I didn't spend any money on it,' Andy said. 'I nicked it from work. And…you might not like it, anyway.'

'Show me.'

Andy felt in the pocket of the coat he'd dropped over the end of the couch when the tree decoration had got properly under way. He held up the slim, rectangular box with some trepidation. It wasn't much of a gift.

'Peace of mind?' he offered softly.

The laughter and lightness was sucked out of the room so fast Andy cursed himself for even having the idea in the first place, but Gemma, her face completely neutral, took the box and disappeared into the tiny bathroom of the apartment.

She didn't come out.

Andy waited for two minutes and then paced back and forth for another three. These tests only took a minute to cook, didn't they? He knocked on the door.

'You OK?'

He got no answer. Unsure whether to burst in on her, Andy leaned his forehead on the door and that was when he heard it.

A stifled sob.

He threw the door open. Gemma was sitting on the toilet lid, staring at the stick she held in one hand. Her other hand was cradling her forehead. She had tears coursing down her face.

Andy dropped to his knees in front of her and

reached to spread his hands and hold as much of Gemma as he could grasp.

'It's OK,' he told her. 'We'll cope.'

But Gemma shook her head, shaking with sobs. Andy waited and finally, she started to force some words out.

'I thought…you know…I thought if the worst happened, it wasn't that big a deal… Lots of people have terminations because…they can't afford a baby…or it's just totally the wrong time in their lives…'

The chill that ran down Andy's spine made it hard to stay silent and keep listening but Gemma wasn't finished yet.

'But then it hit me…you know? This is a *baby*, Andy. *Our* baby…and I just can't…'

'No…of course you can't.' His relief was astonishingly strong. Andy stood up, gathering Gemma in his arms. Holding her tight.

'It's over,' Gemma sobbed against his chest. 'My career. All those dreams…'

'No,' he said fiercely. 'They're not over. I won't

let that happen, Gem. We're in this together. We'll make it work.'

'But…*how*?'

'I don't know yet.' Andy took a deep breath, thinking fast. 'We're going to be specialist registrars. We'll have more defined hours. We can juggle shifts and use the hospital day-care facilities. I'll make sure I do half the chores. My parents would help us with a deposit for a bigger apartment. A house, even.'

'But you swore you would never accept financial help from your family. You wanted to make it on your own.'

'This is more important. We all have to compromise sometimes in life. It'll be temporary. Just like how hard it might be for the first year or so of having a baby. It's temporary. You have to look at the bigger picture.'

Gemma seemed calmer now. 'What's that?'

'Us.' Andy pulled back far enough to meet Gemma's gaze. 'I love you,' he said softly. 'I want to be with you for the rest of my life. I want us to have a family together. Maybe we're getting pushed into it a bit faster than would have been ideal but…God, Gemma. I love you *so* much…'

'I love you, too.'

'Marry me.' The words came from nowhere but the moment they left his lips Andy knew they were exactly what he wanted to say. What he wanted to happen, with all his heart. Gemma was staring at him, open-mouthed. 'Please?' he added.

She was still staring. He could almost see the whirl of her thoughts. The fear of how hard it would be now to achieve the career she wanted so much. Trying to process the concept of marriage and family when it had been the last thing she'd wanted. What had she always said? That she'd spent virtually her whole life being a parent to her younger sister and it would be a very long time before she wanted to go there again. But mixed in with the negative, difficult thoughts Andy could also see something glowing. Her trust in him.

Her love.

'I could go down on one knee,' he offered with a crooked smile.

Gemma's lips twitched. 'I think you already did that when I was sitting on the loo.' She bit her lip. 'Oh, my God, Andy. You just proposed to me in the *bathroom*.'

'Easily fixed.' Andy led her back into their small living area. The chocolate reindeer on the top of their joke of a Christmas tree was hanging upside down now.

But it gave Andy inspiration.

'Don't move,' he told Gemma.

It was there somewhere, he knew it was. In a box at the back of the crowded wardrobe in the bedroom. Amongst a collection of old snapshots and Scout badges and odd treasures that marked important milestones in his life. When he found it, he went back to Gemma and held it aloft triumphantly.

'Remember this?'

Gemma smiled but her eyes filled with tears again as she nodded.

Andy kept hold of the piece of plastic mistletoe.

He moved his hand so that it was above Gemma's head. And then he kissed her. Maybe he couldn't put how much he loved her into the right words but he could *show* her.

Her eyes were still closed when he finally broke the tender kiss. When she opened them, they were as misty as her smile.

'Yes,' she whispered. 'I'd love to marry you.' Her smile wobbled. 'Laura's coming next week to talk about *her* wedding. She's the one who actually wants to have a baby soon. She's not going to believe this. I don't think I believe it.'

Andy kissed her again. He believed it. He knew it wasn't going to be easy but the confidence that they would make it through and that it was the right thing to do was growing. He just needed to convince Gemma.

'Let's have dinner,' he suggested. 'Don't know about you, but I'm absolutely *starving.*' He rescued the upside-down reindeer and gave it to Gemma. 'Dessert.' He grinned.

She smiled back and that was the moment

Andy knew that everything would be all right. They could do this.

Together.

CHAPTER SIX

THE yearning wouldn't go away.

If anything, standing in front of the ward Christmas tree and letting memories from the past out of their locked cage had made it worse.

Andy could feel that moment when he'd proposed to Gemma as if it had just happened. The confidence of his love for her that he'd been so sure would carry them through anything life could throw at them. The excitement at the thought of being a father, which had been so unexpected because he'd known that Gemma would have resisted starting a family for as long as possible. The sheer joy of her acceptance of his proposal... Knowing that he'd won. He'd found the holy grail of winning a partner for life.

Something that huge and that real couldn't have simply faded into nothingness, could it?

Bled to death in the wake of the trauma of Gemma leaving him?

No.

Those few minutes in front of the Christmas tree had let Andy know without a shadow of a doubt that it was all still there.

On his side, at least.

But what about Gemma? There'd been that moment earlier this evening when he'd thought he could see something that suggested it hadn't changed for her either. Not below the surface.

That look in her eyes when Hazel had dropped the verbal bombshell that Sophie might be going to die.

He hadn't imagined that link. The kind of connection that only came from knowing somebody else almost as well as you knew yourself.

If it had just been the knowledge it would have little more than a shared memory but there had been something much bigger in that shared glance. An expectation of trust, because that was what was being offered.

And somehow, putting those components together had added up to much, much more than he would have expected the total to be. The combination of a shared past and continued trust could only be fused by love.

Yes. If he chose to interpret that moment with an open mind—or rather heart—he might believe that beneath the landslide of rubble they'd piled onto their relationship and tried to bury it with there was still a rock-solid foundation. It was possible that Gemma still loved him.

As much as he still loved her?

Could he go there with some emotional rescue dogs and sniff out some signs of life beneath that rubble?

Did he want to?

Maybe he didn't but maybe he had no choice.

He'd never moved on, had he? He'd tried. God knew, he'd tried so many times but the initial flash of attraction he might have discovered with other women soon flickered out. As much as he desperately wanted to find them, the channels that created the kind of connection he'd had with Gemma didn't seem to exist with anybody else.

Without any conscious decision, Andy found his feet moving him back towards Gemma's room. The route took him past the nurses' station.

'Andy?' Lisa was sitting at the desk beside the phone. She looked up, about to say something, but then frowned. 'You OK?'

Oh…help. Did his disturbed emotional state show on his face that clearly? 'I'm fine,' he said. 'What's up?'

'Two things. You remember Chantelle Simms?'

'Of course. Three-year-old with severe abdominal pain and diarrhoea. No fever, nothing showing on a scan and normal bloods. We discharged her this morning.'

'Yes, well, she's just been brought back into Emergency. Screaming with pain and the mother is beside herself. They're having trouble calming either of them down but when they have, they're going to send her back up.'

Andy was frowning now. 'What on earth did we miss? She seemed absolutely fine when we sent her home this morning. And her mum was so relieved that they didn't have to stay in for Christmas. What was the mum's name again?'

'Deirdre.'

'Hmm.' Something was nagging at the back of Andy's mind. She'd been a young, single mother. So worried about her daughter.

'She's all I have in the world, Dr Baxter. I couldn't bear it if something happened to her.'

There'd been tears. Uncontrolled sobbing, in fact, that had needed a fair bit of reassurance and shoulder patting.

A perfectly normal parental reaction to having a child who was clearly unwell. But...

'The other thing...' Lisa was reaching for a piece of paper. 'Results on the Gillespie baby have come through. Looks like it's not measles or meningitis or anything nasty.'

Andy scanned the results himself. 'Thank goodness for that. I guess the ear infection is definitely the culprit.'

'Her temperature was well down when I checked her vital signs a wee while ago. Will you discharge her?'

Andy glanced at his watch. 'It's after midnight,' he observed. 'It would be a bit rough to send Gemma home with five kids to try and settle again.'

'Mmm.' Lisa's tone was neutral but her gaze was steady. Curious.

'She might want to go, of course.' Andy did his best to keep his own tone just as neutral. 'I'll give her the option.' He turned away, before Lisa could try and read anything more into the situation. 'Give me a call as soon as Chantelle and her mum arrive on the ward.'

There was a brief period of absolute peace when Gemma had finally settled Sophie back into the bassinette. For a long minute or two she simply stood there in the midst of this little tribe of sleeping children and listened to the sound of their breathing.

Feeling the tension of this extraordinarily difficult night ebbing to a point where it could become quite manageable.

And then there was a soft tap at the door and it opened and there was Andy.

'Hi...' His smile seemed tentative in the half-light and his voice was too quiet to read anything into his tone. 'How's it going?'

Gemma knew her own smile was also tentative but she was struggling here. With an echo of that relief that Andy's presence had brought with it from the moment she'd first seen him again in Queen Mary's waiting room. With the yearning for it to be more than what it could possibly be now. With...*missing* him so much.

It shouldn't be this hard, she told herself in those split seconds of trying to pull herself together enough to give him a coherent response and not just burst into tears and throw herself into his arms or something.

Missing Andy was just a part of life for her now, wasn't it?

In the beginning, she had missed him in the way you might miss a limb that had been torn off in a dreadful accident. An unbearably painful injury and, even though you knew the limb was no longer there, you could *feel* it. And you'd go to do things that required its presence, forgetting for a split second that it was no longer available. And with the realisation of the way things really were now would come a fresh wave of that excruciating pain.

But nobody could live like that for ever and, as trite as it sounded, time was a great healer. Well, a pretty good one, anyway. Protective mechanisms like blocking emails, not picking up those early phone calls and deleting the voice mail before listening had also helped.

And, at some point, it had become the safe and sensible thing to continue to do. Contacting Andy would be to invite news that he'd moved on. That he had found someone who could give him all the things that she hadn't been able to. That might have been the object of the exercise, of course, but Gemma wasn't ready to hear about it.

Maybe she never would be.

Because, while she thought she'd become used to missing Andy, she'd been wrong.

And being this close, where she could see him

and hear him and even touch him, but what they'd once had was gone.

And…oh, God…she missed that *so* much and there was no way she could tell him that because he'd moved on with his life. He had a career he clearly loved and he was admired and respected by his colleagues. He might have someone else in his private life. He seemed to have found peace, at least, and he didn't deserve her coming back and damaging the good space he was in.

'It's all good,' she heard herself whispering finally, in response to Andy's query. 'They're all asleep.'

Andy was looking around the room. Slowly. His gaze rested on each child and lingered longest on Sophie. He looked about to speak but then beckoned Gemma. She followed him out of the room.

'Don't want to wake anybody,' Andy said. 'Unless you do?'

Gemma blinked. 'Why would I want to do that?'

'We've got the lab results back. There's no reason to keep Sophie or any of the other children in any kind of quarantine. It's not measles.'

'Thank goodness.'

'And it's certainly not…anything else that's serious.' Andy's hesitation might not have been noticeable to anybody else but it shouted a single word to Gemma.

Her indrawn breath was a gulp. She had to look away. To break that connection that had the potential to open such deep, deep wounds.

'So…' Andy cleared his throat. 'If you wanted, you could take all the children home, but…'

Gemma's gaze flew back to meet his. There was a 'but'? A potential complication for Sophie?

'I thought you might like to let them sleep until morning. It would be a shame to start Christmas Day with overtired and unhappy children, wouldn't it?'

'Would that be OK?'

Andy nodded. 'I have a feeling that both I and my registrar will be far too busy to sign the discharge papers before morning.'

'Oh…' The decision was a no-brainer. 'Thanks, Andy.'

'No problem.' He cleared his throat again and glanced at his watch. 'I'm going to hang around for a bit because there's a re-admission coming up from Emergency soon.' His tone was both confident and casual but the glance he sent Gemma held a question that he seemed unsure of even asking. 'Would you…like a coffee?'

What Gemma really needed was a few hours' sleep so that she would be able to take care of the children in the morning so a stimulant like coffee would not be a good idea.

But that wasn't what Andy was offering, was it?

He was asking if she'd like the chance to talk. To him. Alone? Her heart gave a thump and picked up speed. This was unexpected. She'd had no way of preparing for such a conversation. Did Andy want to know something in particular or did he feel the need to go over old, painful ground? And, if he did, could she bring herself to refuse?

There were things she would like to know herself. Like whether there *was* someone special in his life that his colleagues didn't know about.

Like how he was feeling seeing her again like this. Had he missed her the way she'd missed him? Was he aware of the sheet of seemingly unbreakable glass between them that could move and reshape itself to provide a barrier for even physical touch?

'I'd l—' The word died on Gemma's lips. *Like* wasn't really an appropriate expectation in accepting this invitation. *Love* even less so. 'Um… yes,' she said quietly instead.

'Come with me.' Andy turned. 'I'll ask Lisa to get one of the nurses to keep an eye on the children. We can make a drink in the kitchen and then take it into my office.'

He'd done it now.

Engineered a situation that could well make everything far harder than it needed to be.

He'd taken Gemma away from the children. Removed himself from any distraction or the chaperonage of colleagues.

He'd brought her into a private space. Not even a neutral space. This was his office. More than a home away from home because the apartment he lived in was merely a space to exist when he was away from work.

This office was his real home because home was where the heart was. It was here that he kept his favourite books and CDs and...oh, yeah...

How could he have forgotten that photo on his desk? The one of he and Gemma in the park that day. Standing in several inches of snow, kissing beneath the frosted branches of an old, weeping elm tree. A photo that had been taken on a day's leave that they had laughingly deemed their honeymoon. When they'd gone to Cambridge to tell his parents that a new generation of the Baxter family was on its way.

Maybe Gemma couldn't see the photograph from where she was sitting in the leather armchair reserved for visitors. Andy pulled the chair from behind his desk, both to sit without the barrier of furniture between them but also to distract Gemma from spotting the photograph.

He really didn't want her to see it. She'd moved on with her life, having chosen to leave him behind. He didn't want her to know that he hadn't managed to do the same. He didn't want to make himself so vulnerable all over again.

'So...' Andy took a sip of his coffee, watching Gemma over the rim of the mug. 'Here we are, then.'

'Mmm.' Gemma was staring at the liquid in her mug as though trying to decide whether she wanted to drink it or not. Her body language suggested she felt as awkward as Andy suddenly did.

The silence that fell seemed impossible to break but then Gemma raised her chin for just an instant to meet his eyes before she looked down again.

'Sorry,' she said.

Why was she sorry? Because seeing him again was the last thing she had wanted?

Andy felt his breath leave his chest in a sigh. If someone had asked him that morning, he might have said that seeing Gemma was the last thing *he* would want, but, now that it had happened, he knew it would have been a lie. A huge lie.

'I'm not,' he said quietly. 'It's good to see you, Gem.'

Her face lifted sharply, revealing a startled gaze instead of an apologetic one. She hadn't expected him to say that but something was shining through the surprise. Hope?

'You're looking good,' Andy added with a smile.

Gemma gave an incredulous huff. 'Are you kidding? I'm like the walking dead. I've never been as tired as I've been in the last six months. Not even when we were doing a hundred-plus hours a week as junior doctors.'

'Running on adrenaline,' Andy sympathised. 'It catches up with you eventually.'

His gaze held hers for a heartbeat longer. Did she remember the rare occasions that their days off had coincided back then? They'd have such big plans to make the most of the day but, so often, they would end up on the couch, wrapped in each other's arms. Sound asleep. A tangle of limbs like the twins in their shared cot down the corridor.

Andy could actually remember the feel of being that close to Gemma. Hearing the sound of her soft breathing. Feeling the steady thump of her heart. Being aware of the solid security of knowing that he was not, and never would be, alone in the world.

He had to look away but his traitorous glance slid towards that photograph on his desk.

'Yeah…I'm a wreck,' Gemma was saying. 'Haven't been near a hairdresser since I got back. Can't even remember where I left my mascara.'

'You don't need it.' Andy could hear the raw edge in his voice but couldn't stop the words from emerging. 'You never did.'

Another silence fell, just as awkward as the last one. Andy had to break it this time because he could feel Gemma waiting. Poised, as if she didn't know what direction to jump. He was being given the choice here, but he was nowhere near ready to take the unexpected route that was becoming so visible.

So tempting.

And then Andy saw Gemma's gaze rake his desk and get caught by the photograph. Something like panic pushed him forward. He found a bright, casual tone to use.

'What's it like, living in Sydney?' he asked.

The disappointment was absolutely crushing.

It was the kind of question you might ask a complete stranger. Virtually the complete opposite of the last words he'd spoken—telling her that she didn't need to wear mascara.

Reminding her that he'd always thought she was beautiful, even first thing in the morning or after a solid night on call when she'd had no sleep and had felt like a zombie. And...he had *that* photograph on his desk. A reminder of just how close they had once been there in front of him. Every day. Why?

And why had he said something that had brought them so close again and then pushed her away so abruptly by saying something so impersonal?

He needs time, she reminded herself. We both do. Time to get used to breathing the same air again.

'Sydney's great,' she said. 'Gorgeous city.'

'What part do you live in?'

'I had an apartment close to where I worked at Sydney Harbour Hospital.' Gemma emphasised the past tense. 'Top floor of a block and I had a balcony that looked over the Harbour Bridge and the Opera House. Pretty much like a postcard.'

She couldn't read any expression on Andy's face and Gemma knew he had to work hard to appear that impassive. Especially when she'd never had any trouble reading the tiny changes that could happen around his eyes and mouth. She realised she could still read the impassiveness just as easily. He didn't like what he was hearing.

Sure enough, his voice was tightly controlled when he spoke again.

'And the job? Was that perfect, too?'

There was anger behind those words. Hurt. Fair enough. Gemma closed her eyes for a moment.

'I became a consultant radiologist a year ago. Specialising in MRI and ultrasound.'

'Any particular interests?' Andy sounded genuinely interested now. This was safe ground. A professional discussion rather than personal.

'Image-guided procedures,' Gemma responded.

'Like biopsies?'

'And surgeries. I especially like being involved in spinal and neurological cases.'

Andy looked impressed. 'Sounds fascinating. Full on, I bet.'

'Yes. It was.'

He raised an eyebrow. 'Past tense?'

Gemma shrugged. 'For the foreseeable future. And at the rate the technologies change, I doubt that I'll ever catch up again.'

And it didn't matter, she wanted to add. There *were* more important things in life than a high-powered career. She'd learned that the hard way, being thrown in at the deep end as the only living relative for five young orphans. Andy had known it all along, hadn't he?

But how could she tell him that?

If it hadn't taken her so long to learn, they would probably still be together. As an intact family, even.

No…she couldn't go there.

And…it was too late now, anyway.

Wasn't it?

Andy couldn't interpret the look he was getting from Gemma.

Did she think he wouldn't understand how important her career was to her? He almost snorted aloud. It had always been more important than anything else in her life. Including him. He might not like that about her but he'd always understood.

'You could probably get a job here,' he told her. 'There's always a shortage of specialist skills like you have. Part time,' he added, seeing her incredulous expression. 'When you've got childcare organised.'

Gemma was still staring at him. She looked totally lost for words.

'Is…um…money a problem?' How sad that

he felt so uncomfortable asking such a personal question but, if that was what was holding her back, he could help.

Gemma shook her head. 'Not at all. Both Laura and Evan had good life insurance cover. The house is safe and the children will always be well provided for. Financially, I probably never need to work again.'

'But you want to.'

Gemma looked away. 'It's not an option right now. I'm not even thinking about it.'

Really? She'd become the thing she'd sworn she never would be. A full-time stay-at-home mother. And she was OK with that?

The idea was confusing enough to make Andy head for safe territory.

'Is the house the same one? The barn conversion?'

'Yes. Evan made such a fabulous job of it. It's an amazing family home.'

'I remember. He sourced those old beams and stained-glass windows. I helped him shift all those stone slabs for doing the kitchen floor.'

Andy smiled ruefully. 'Don't think my back has ever been quite the same.'

'They did heaps more while I've been away, too. Added on a new wing after the twins came along. And Laura somehow found time to create a huge garden. You could just about stock a supermarket from the vegetable patch and orchard.'

'There was a lot of land to play with, that's for sure.'

'A lot of it is in paddocks. There's a few pet sheep and Hazel's got a pony. Lots of hens, too. Laura sold eggs to the neighbours.'

'Sounds…idyllic.'

Andy could have kicked himself as the word came out. The situation was so far from idyllic…for everybody involved. The children had lost their parents. Gemma had lost her sister and brother-in-law and she'd had to leave the career she loved so much. And maybe she'd had to leave more than her career behind in Sydney. The man he'd heard berating her in the reception area had clearly been expecting to go on a date with Gemma but did that necessarily mean she hadn't left someone special behind in Australia?

'Sorry,' he muttered. 'I didn't mean that to sound...I don't know...flippant.'

'It's OK. It *is* idyllic. It was Laura's dream home and lifestyle and I intend to keep it alive for her children, no matter what.'

'Family,' Andy murmured. 'That's what it's all about, isn't it?'

'Yes.'

He could see Gemma swallow hard and take a deep breath. Open her mouth to say something that was obviously difficult.

'What about you, Andy? Are you...? I mean, is there someone...um... Have you got...?'

What? A substitute for the family he could have had with her? Andy waited for her to finish the question, his heart sinking. He didn't want to talk about himself. There was nothing to tell Gemma but too much he wanted to say.

And maybe he could talk to her now. Really talk. They were closed off from the world here and he could feel the strangeness of being alone with Gemma again wearing off. Every time his eyes met hers, he could feel barriers cracking. Chunks of them falling away, even. Could he tell her the truth? And, if he did, where would that lead them?

But neither of them got the chance to say anything else. A knock on the door heralded the appearance of a nurse.

'Lisa said to tell you that Chantelle's arrived on the ward. Her mother's refusing to let your registrar admit her. She wants you.' From somewhere down the corridor came the faint wail of a frightened child.

'I'll be right there.' Andy pushed himself to his feet. The spell was broken and the outside world had intruded, and maybe that was for the best. He left his coffee where it was on the desk. He'd only taken that one sip and it would be stone cold by the time he got back.

Gemma hadn't drunk hers either.

'Stay here and finish your coffee if you like,' he told her. 'I'll come back and…maybe we could talk some more.'

Gemma gave him another one of those surprised looks. 'If you want to,' she said. Her unfinished question was still hanging in the air.

'I do,' Andy said quietly.

But Gemma didn't seem to be listening to him any more. The silent question on her face was directed at the nurse.

'It's not one of yours crying, don't worry,' the nurse reassured her.

But Gemma was on her feet now and Andy could feel the tension in her body. She was clearly still listening to the baby cry and needed to make sure it wasn't one of her own.

She was scared, Andy realised. Terrified that something horrible was going to happen to one of those precious kids.

Of course she was.

He had to reach out and touch her. To offer his own reassurance. To let her know that he understood.

Really understood.

And when Gemma tilted her chin and met his gaze, he could see that his message was being received with all the nuances that came from their past.

Just like him, she was listening to that cry and thinking about Max.

CHAPTER SEVEN

Christmas: six years ago

'CALL for you, Gemma. Outside line.'

'Thank you.' Gemma dumped the armload of patient notes she was carrying on the desk and reached for the phone. 'Hi hon, how's it going?'

There was surprised laughter on the line. 'How did you know it was me?'

Gemma groaned. 'I didn't. And I didn't think it *was* you, Laura. I thought it was Andy. He was going to call and let me know how Max is.'

'Is he sick?'

'Bit sniffly and grumpy this morning. Probably just a cold coming on but he had me up a few times in the night.'

'Oh, no...poor you. That's all you need when you've got to get up and go to work.'

'Worse for Andy if he's been unsettled all

day. There's no guarantee he'll get any sleep on night shift.'

'Poor him, too. Can't believe he has to do a night shift on Christmas Eve.'

'We figured it's a small price to pay for having been able to juggle our rosters so well. Things will get easier in the new year once Max starts day care for more than one day a week.'

'And you've definitely got tomorrow off? You're not going to get called in at the last minute or something?'

'No way. Not when we're going to see your new kitchen in action for the first time. That Aga is going to cook the perfect turkey or there'll be some serious questions being asked.'

Laura laughed. 'Fingers crossed. I'm doing my best. Oh…I can't wait, Gem. Max and Hazel are old enough to know what's going on now. They'll be able to *play* together. It's going to be a real, family Christmas. Dream-come-true stuff…'

'You're not going to start crying on me, are you?'

The sniff was noisy enough to make Gemma wince. 'No-o-o…I'm just…so happy.'

'I will be, too, as soon as I get away from here. I've got a full ward round to get done first, though, so I'll have to go.'

'OK…but…'

'But?' There was an urgency in Laura's tone that made Gemma pause. 'What's wrong?'

'I'm not supposed to tell you yet but…I'm going to *burst* if I don't.'

'Don't do that. It would be messy and I have no idea how to cook turkeys.' Gemma heard another sniff. And then a very happy sigh. Where had she heard that before?

'Oh, my God, Laura…are you *pregnant* again?'

'I think I might be. I *hope* so.'

'Fingers crossed, then.' Gemma closed her eyes as she shook her head. 'Rather you than me.'

'Maybe it'll be a boy this time. So Max won't have to play with girls all his life.'

'Good thinking.'

'You could always have another one…' Laura

suggested breathlessly. 'Remember how fun it was when we both had babies at the same time?'

'Fun? Are you kidding? It was a logistical nightmare. One that's only just starting to get manageable. No...' Gemma glanced at her watch. 'I've got to go, Laura. I'll see you in the morning.'

'Are you mad at me?'

'No, of course not. I'm delighted for you. I'm delighted that you're going to provide a whole bunch of cousins for Max so I won't have to feel guilty about him being an only child. But I *have* to go. Now. Love you. 'Bye.'

Gemma eyed the phone after she'd hung up on Laura. She got as far as dialling the outside line, intending to call Andy and see how things were going at home. But what if he'd just got Max down for his nap and was finally grabbing the hour or two's sleep he must desperately need? Gemma put the phone down again. With a resigned sigh she picked up the big stack of patient notes and headed out into the ward.

There were fourteen patients to check on. Some

would need physical examinations and some would need results chased up and possibly further investigations ordered. She might even have to call the consultant in if there was anything she was really concerned about. All these patients and probably a few family members would need a chance to talk to their doctor. If she was really, really lucky, she would be able to get through it all in four hours or so.

And then she could go home to the two men in her life and start Christmas.

How good was that going to be?

There were no flowers allowed in the respiratory ward Gemma was working in at the moment so the staff had made up for a year's worth of lacking colour by going to town with non-allergenic Christmas decorations. Tinsel and banners and multicoloured baubles were tied to every handle, strung across doorways and decorated bed ends and trolleys. With a smile, Gemma broke off a piece of bright green tinsel and tied it around the short ponytail taming her hair.

Then she went to collect her junior houseman

and a nurse from the staff kitchen. If Andy called she would interrupt the round for a couple of minutes. If he didn't, that meant everything was fine and she'd wait until she got home to catch up.

Gemma and Andy were still living in a basement flat but this one had two bedrooms, a bigger living area and even two chairs and a microscopic patch of grass outside. It also cost nearly twice as much as their first flat had but, with them both working full time finally, it was getting much easier to manage the finances. They were at last saving for a deposit on a house of their own and the plan was for them to have moved by next Christmas.

It was nearly six p.m. by the time Gemma arrived home. Andy was due to start his night shift at nine p.m. so they would have a good couple of hours together before he had to head off.

'Hi, honey…I'm home,' she called as she closed the front door behind her. It was a standing joke but, in the silence that followed her greeting, Gemma bit her lip. It didn't always produce a smile. Maybe Andy had had a rough day, in which case the sing-song announcement of her arrival to take over the parenting duties could be met with some built-up resentment. It was something she'd had to work on herself in those early days when she'd had the lion's share of caring for Max.

The tiny hallway of the flat was no more than a place to hang coats and keys. It finished with a bathroom at the end. A door to the left led to the main bedroom. The second bedroom opened off that and would probably get turned into a walk-in wardrobe by a future owner. A door to the right led to the open-plan living room and kitchen with the door that opened to the tiny, below street level courtyard.

At this time of the evening Max would be due for his bath but the door to the bathroom was closed so that obviously wasn't happening. Gemma could feel a knot of tension in her stomach now. Playing with Max in the bath was such a treat it was the reward for anything not so good that had happened during the day. The time afterwards, with Max in his fluffy pyjamas, smelling sweetly of baby powder and ready for cuddles and bedtime, was the best of family time. It was when they both knew that the struggle was worth it. That the bond they all had was precious.

Maybe Andy was still feeding Max his dinner but it was too quiet for that to be happening. Max loved his food. He was always messy and noisy, especially when he had his favourite wooden spoon to bang on the tray of his high chair.

And why hadn't the lights been turned on? It was pitch black outside now. And freezing. But the shiver that ran through Gemma as she flung her coat onto a hook didn't feel like it was caused by the cold. The door to the living room was slightly ajar so it made no sound as Gemma pushed it open.

There was a source of light after all. The twinkling lights on the Christmas tree shone green and red and blue in turn. A real Christmas tree this year, albeit an artificial one. Yesterday they had taken far too many photographs of Max sitting beneath it wearing a Santa hat and looking impossibly cute amongst the brightly wrapped parcels.

It took less than the time to draw a breath to see what was going on. Andy was sound asleep on the couch, one arm trailing to leave an up-turned palm on the rug, the fingers curled gently. Right beside that hand was the baby monitor so that he would hear the moment Max woke up from his nap.

Gemma's heart sank. Andy must have been desperate to let Max have such a late nap and it meant that she would be lucky to get him back to bed this side of midnight after he'd had his dinner and bath. She couldn't berate Andy for it, though. They did what they had to do as far as coping with parenting and they had a pact to support each other a hundred per cent.

Gemma flicked on a lamp and then the kitchen light. She filled the jug and plugged it in. Andy was going to need a bucket of coffee before setting off to work.

Neither the light nor the sound of her moving around woke Andy up so Gemma went and knelt beside the couch, intending to wake him with a kiss on his cheek.

She simply knelt there for a long moment, however. Andy looked *so* tired. He hadn't shaved today and his jaw was dark enough to make the rest of face look pale. Even in sleep, she could see the weary furrows etched into his forehead and around his eyes and Gemma felt guilty. If she hadn't been so hell-bent on keeping her career on track, she could have made life so much easier for both of them for this early stage of family life but no…she'd worked until she'd been eight and a half months pregnant and then she'd gone back to work when Max had been only six weeks old.

And Andy had kept his promise of making parenthood an equally shared venture. Done more than his share quite often, in fact, and had never argued over some of the big issues, like stopping breastfeeding so they could share night feeds and remove a looming hassle from her return to work.

Yep. He was a hero, all right. Gemma lifted her hand and gently brushed a lock of unruly hair back from Andy's forehead. The sudden rush of tenderness almost brought tears to her eyes. While having a baby and now a boisterous toddler in their lives had covered a lot of the romance with things like dirty nappies and broken sleep, the underlying love they had for each other had become stronger because of it. Right then, Gemma vowed to try and make life just a bit easier for Andy. Or, at least, to show him, more often, how much she cared about him.

The touch of her hand had been enough to jump-start Andy's journey to consciousness. With his eyes still firmly closed, his lips curled in a smile and his hand came up from the floor to catch Gemma's. He pulled her closer, turning his head and she willingly bent down to kiss his lips.

'Mmm...you're home early...' he murmured.

'Hardly. It's half past six.'

Andy's eyes shot open. *'What?'*

Gemma froze at his horrified tone. 'How long have you been asleep?'

'I put Max down for his nap after lunch.' Andy was pulling himself into a sitting position. With a groan he covered his face with his hands and massaged his forehead. 'It would have been about one o'clock.'

He'd been asleep for five and half hours? Gemma still felt frozen. Oh…God…she was too scared to go and check. Memories of Max as a tiny baby, so soundly asleep that you couldn't see whether he was breathing or not, came back to haunt her. But sixteen months was way too late to be worrying about cot death, wasn't it?

As if to reassure her, there was a crackle from the baby monitor. A snuffling sound and then a grunt. Gemma was half way to being on her feet when a new sound was transmitted.

It was a child's cry but it was not a sound she had ever heard Max making before. Or any child, for that matter. It was a weird, high-pitched keening that made her blood run cold.

Andy was on his feet now as well. Gemma saw the Adam's apple in his throat move as he swallowed hard. His face went white.

With a muttered oath he overtook Gemma as they both rushed into their son's bedroom.

* * *

This was a nightmare.

He was supposed to be in the emergency department of the Queen Mary Infirmary as a senior registrar on night duty, not as the parent of a seriously sick child.

Somebody's cellphone was ringing with the tune of 'Jingle Bells'. A young female member of the domestic staff went past with a mop and bucket and a headband sporting reindeer antlers with flashing lights on the top. The nurse doing triage was wearing a Santa hat identical to the one they'd been taking photos of Max wearing last night.

How could anyone be thinking of Christmas right now?

It had ceased to be of any relevance whatsoever from the moment they had turned the light on in Max's bedroom and seen his flushed, feverish-looking face. The fontanelle on the top of his head had been bulging and tense but what had terrified both Andy and Gemma most had been finding the rash on his abdomen and chest.

Just a few spots but they had been bright red and refused to blanch with pressure.

There had been no time to wait for an ambulance and neither of them had seemed to notice that they were breaking the law by having Max wrapped in a blanket in Gemma's arms instead of being in his car seat as they'd rushed him to hospital.

Arriving here—to the expertise and technology geared to save lives should have been a comfort but it only marked the real beginning of the nightmare. Gemma had tears streaming down her face as she helped two nurses hold Max as still as possible, curled up on his side so that the senior ED consultant could perform a lumbar puncture. It was an agonisingly slow wait for the drops of clear fluid to be collected into several different tubes.

Finally, it was over, and Gemma was allowed to pick Max up and cuddle him for a minute.

'We'll get IV access and start the antibiotics now,' the consultant said. 'I'll get a bed organised in the PICU.' He picked up a chart. 'Run through it again for me. He was symptom-free yesterday?'

Gemma rocked Max, who was looking drowsy now. 'He had an unsettled night but he wasn't running a temperature. I thought he might be getting a new tooth or something.'

'And this morning?'

'He was just a bit…irritable. A slight sniffle, that's all. Like the very start of a head cold.'

'He was rubbing his ear at lunchtime,' Andy added. 'He's had ear infections before so I assumed that's what it was. I gave him some paracetamol and he settled for a nap without a fuss.'

'And he slept for five and a half hours.' The consultant's tone held a grim edge. 'How long does he normally nap?'

'An hour. An hour and a half if we're lucky.' It was Gemma who answered. Andy could feel her gaze on him. He swallowed hard.

'I fell asleep as well,' he admitted. 'I have to, when I'm working nights and looking after Max during the day. I didn't think to set an alarm be-cause…'

Because he'd never needed to. He'd had the monitor right beside him and he knew he'd wake at the first squeak. Maybe Max had made a sound at some stage but he'd slipped into such a deep sleep by then it had simply become part of a dream. This was his fault. He should have spotted the signs. Had Max in here with some powerful antibiotics running through his veins hours ago.

Because every minute counted in the war against bacterial meningitis.

'When did he last pass any urine?'

'I changed his nappy before lunch.'

'It's still dry now,' Gemma added quietly.

The consultant had finished scribbling his notes. He turned to his registrar, who was still filling in the forms for the CSF and blood sam-ples collected. 'Make sure you've covered mi-croscopy, culture, protein and glucose analysis. And put a rush on getting the results.'

'Will do.'

'Go up to PICU with the Baxters. I'll come

up as soon as I've got a minute. Make sure that plasma and urine electrolytes are carefully monitored and fluids restricted until we see some signs of recovery.'

Recovery.

That was the magic word.

The only gift that mattered this Christmas. Gemma had heard the word as well. Huge eyes in a pale face searched out and locked on his. Andy took a step closer and put his arm around both Gemma and Max. He might be powerless in protecting his family from what was happening but at least he could hold them close.

'We'll start a standard combination antibiotic regime immediately,' the consultant was telling them both. 'And then we'll transfer you upstairs.' He paused and Andy knew that this was the moment to offer a family reassurance if there was any to be had.

'We'd better start both of you on prophylactic antibiotics as well.' The consultant's voice was sympathetic. 'I'm really sorry, but this looks like a clear case of meningococcal disease.'

Recovery was looking further away instead of closer as the hours ticked past and Christmas Eve became Christmas Day.

'He's in septic shock,' the PICU consultant told them. 'We're going to intubate and get him onto a ventilator.'

The rash was rapidly evolving. Instead of the tiny red pinpricks on Max's chest and abdomen, he now had a rash over his entire body. And it wasn't just little spots. They seemed to be joining together in places to make ugly, dark stains on his skin that looked like inkblots.

He wasn't just put on the ventilator. Their precious little boy had to have a nasogastric tube placed. And a urinary catheter. A larger-bore IV line was inserted as well so that therapy to control his blood pressure and electrolyte abnormalities could be administered.

'Order some fresh frozen plasma, too,' the consultant told his registrar. 'It's highly likely we've got coagulation issues happening.'

For any parents this was terrifying. For Gemma and Andy, who could understand all the terminology and the reasons that particular tests were being ordered or procedures were being done, it was even worse. They knew exactly how dangerous an illness this was. They knew what needed to be done and could have done it themselve... on someone else's child.

But this was their son. Their only child. And even if there hadn't been rules about treating close relatives yourselves, the emotional involvement rendered them incapable of being relied on for objective analysis or the ability to perform invasive procedures.

For a short time, after the initial rush to get ventilation started and new drugs including narcotic pain relief on board, there was a lull in the number of people hovering over Max and disturbing his body with different procedures or tests.

Andy and Gemma could sit beside the bed, holding each other's hands tightly. Almost too scared to breathe.

For a long time neither of them spoke. It was Andy who broke the silence.

'I'm sorry, Gem.'

'What for?'

'I fell asleep. I should have spotted this so much earlier.'

The extra squeeze on his hand was comforting. 'You can't blame yourself. You were exhausted. You have to nap when Maxie's asleep. If he didn't wake up, then of course you wouldn't have either.'

'I know, but—'

'If we're going to go down the "Who can we blame?" track, what about me? I knew he was sniffly this morning and I still went off to work. I'm the mother who wouldn't stay at home full time, which was why you were exhausted in the first place. It's my fault as much as yours.'

'It's nobody's fault,' Andy had to admit. 'It's…' His throat was closing. Clogging with tears that were too deep to come out. 'It's bloody awful, that's what.'

'He can fight this. I remember a case when I was doing Paeds. A nine-month-old girl who had it as badly as this. Full septic shock and organ failure and she was on ventilation for ten days. She ended up having to have surgical debridement of the skin on her fingers and toes but she survived. Nothing got…got amputated…'

Gemma's voice disintegrated into a choked sob and she lowered her head and began sobbing silently, her pain and fear almost palpable things. Andy put his arm around her shoulders and drew her close enough for her head to rest on his chest. The position they still slept in by choice. He rubbed her back gently in big circles.

A nurse came close. 'Your sister's here,' she said. 'Laura Gillespie? I've put her in the relatives' room. Do you want to go and see her?'

Andy's hold on Gemma tightened. They couldn't leave Max by himself even if he was unconscious. He didn't want Gemma out of reach either. He had to hold them all close together. As a family.

But Laura was family, too. A combination of both sister and child to Gemma after she'd practically raised her. She was also the mother of Max's best friend and cousin, Hazel. They couldn't shut her out.

'Bring her in,' he suggested. 'And…she and her family had better start the prophylactic anti-biotics, too. They've spent time with us over the last few days.'

They were supposed to be spending the day to-gether tomorrow. Celebrating Christmas.

Laura came in, wearing a gown and mask. She stopped abruptly when she got close to the bed and uttered a soft cry of horror.

It had the effect of showing both Andy and Gemma the scene through fresh eyes.

Max's tiny, naked body lay on the top of the bed, criss-crossed by the wires connecting elec-trodes to the monitoring equipment. Numerous IV ports were splashes of colour amongst the clear tubing and white tape. He had tubes in his nose and his mouth and a blood-pressure cuff, which looked far too big, covering an upper arm.

The most shocking thing, however, was the discolouration of his skin. The mottling of the dreadful rash as it spread and intensified.

Laura couldn't cope. Her voice was anguished as she excused herself only minutes later.

'I'll be right outside. Come and get me if...'

Andy nodded. He would go and get her if there was something she could do to help. Or if things got any worse.

Things did get worse within the next couple of hours despite treatment that was as aggressive as this awful disease. Constant monitoring and adjustments to the drug regime were made but Max's blood pressure continued to drop. His renal function declined and it became harder to keep oxygen saturation levels up to an acceptable range.

Worst of all, his little feet and hands were showing marked changes in their colour. The inkblots expanded and darkened until the skin looked almost black. The medical team fought a valiant battle but somewhere just before dawn they knew they had lost. The tubes and wires were taken off and the parents were left alone with their child for the final minutes of his life.

The first stages of grief were a curious phenomenon for Gemma. It was Andy who cried first—great racking sobs of unbearable pain—but she felt completely numb. As though she was sleepwalking through a nightmare that would have to end at some point but not yet.

She held her son as he took his last breath and she had Andy holding them both. It was almost a rerun of the night they'd first met and yet it couldn't have been more different. They hadn't even known each other then and now they had a bond that was so strong it seemed as if nothing could ever break it.

Even this?

Andy didn't seem to think so. When they finally had to leave Max behind, he put his arms around Gemma and held her so tightly she couldn't breathe.

'We'll get through this,' he promised, in a broken whisper. 'Somehow, we're going to get through this together.'

Laura had been distraught. They'd had to call Evan and tell him to come and get her in his work van because there was no way she could drive herself home. She had wanted Gemma and Andy to come with her but couldn't persuade them.

'We need time together,' Gemma told her sister. 'In our own home.'

Only maybe that hadn't been the best idea because walking into the house and feeling how empty it was without Max destroyed Andy all over again and he sat on the couch, his head in his hands, sobbing.

Still Gemma couldn't cry. She knew it would come and when it did she would fall into a pit of grief that would be terrifying in its depth but she was still in that protective, trance-like state.

She walked around the apartment, touching things. The floppy-eared rabbit toy that had been such a favourite. Why hadn't they remembered to take that to the hospital with them? The presents were still under the tree. They were all for Max. What should she do with them now? Brushing loose strands of hair back from her face, she felt the length of that stupid green tinsel still tied to her ponytail. She pulled it free and let it drift to the floor.

The kitchen was a mess. Dishes from lunch sat in the sink and the tray of the highchair was covered with what looked like dried-up custard. There were things all over the table, too. Paper and scissors and glue.

Andy had been making a card. He'd printed out one of the photos of Max they'd taken yesterday and had made a Christmas card. Inside, in wobbly writing that was supposed to look like a toddler had written it were the words:

Merry Christmas. I love you Mummy. From Max.

There was something else on the table beside the card. Without thinking, Gemma picked it up and carried it through to the living room. And it was then that the words on the home-made card sank in.

The moment the wall of grief hit her.

Andy was on his feet in an instant. Holding her in his arms. Sinking with her to the floor as they started to face the unthinkable.

It was a long, long time later that Andy noticed Gemma's clenched fist.

'What have you got?'

Gemma uncurled her fingers. She was holding a shared memento that somehow managed to never get lost and to make an appearance every Christmas.

The sad little piece of plastic mistletoe that she'd found in the lift the first night they'd met. The one Andy had held above her head after he'd proposed to her when she'd found out she was pregnant.

There would be no kiss this year. Instead, they simply clung to each other and cried.

CHAPTER EIGHT

THE reassurance that it hadn't been one of 'her' children crying hadn't been enough.

Gemma abandoned her own cup of coffee and went back to their room to find that they were, indeed, all fast asleep.

What was it about sleeping children that tugged so hard at the heartstrings? Maybe it was that perfect skin and a baby's cupid bow of a mouth that took years to change shape. The spread-eagled position that advertised utter relaxation. Or was it the innocence of such young faces that had yet to face the harsh realities of the world?

Except that these children had already faced too much. Sophie knew nothing about it, of course, and even the twins were young enough to have accepted the massive change in their lives but Jamie, and especially Hazel, would always be aware of that sad gap left by having their own parents torn away. And, while Gemma was doing her best to fill the gap, she could never replace a father completely.

Standing there in the semi-darkness, letting her gaze travel from one child to the next and back again, Gemma was overwhelmed by how protective she felt. How much she loved these children. And by the joy of remembering the cuddles and kisses she had received as she'd settled them down tonight. The words the children had said.

I love Aunty Gemma. She's a good mummy.

You're nice, Aunty Gemma. I love you, too.

It's OK. Aunty Gemma's looking after you. She's looking after all of us.

She was. She always would. Always. Oh…help. She had tears running down her cheeks again. Just as well she had lost her mascara but she must still look a mess. With a sniff and a quick scrub at her cheeks Gemma started moving again. Not into the children's room but down towards the bathroom so that she could wash her face and try and make herself look a bit more respectable.

Because it wasn't just the nurse's reassurance about the children that hadn't been enough. The conversation with Andy felt like it had only just begun. That it had been interrupted at a crucial moment even. Andy had invited her to stay and finish her coffee. He'd said he'd come back and that he wanted to talk some more.

Gemma wanted that, too. *So* much.

Despite it being in the early hours of the morning, Gemma found she wasn't alone in the bathroom. While she was splashing her face with some cold water at the basin, a toilet flushed and then the door banged as a young woman came out in a hurry.

'Oh, God, I needed that!' she exclaimed, heading for the basin beside Gemma. 'I've been hanging on for *hours*.'

Gemma glanced sideways as she reached for some paper towels. The woman looked barely more than a teenager. She was wearing leggings and layers of clothing on her upper body but she was painfully thin. She had dark hair that reached her waist and an abundance of silver jewellery that rattled as she moved her hands and dug in an oversized shoulder-bag.

'Rough night, huh?' she said sympathetically.

'Oh, man…you've got no idea.' The girl didn't look at Gemma. She had pulled a mascara wand from the bag that was balanced precariously on the edge of the basin. She leaned forward to peer at herself in the mirror. 'How awful is it to have to come into a *hospital* on Christmas Eve? We'll be in here for Christmas *Day*.'

The words struck an odd note because attending to her eyelashes seemed to be the most important thing on this girl's mind. Gemma took another glance at her own blotchy face, dismissed the reflection and screwed up the paper towels to drop them into the bin.

'They make it special,' she told the girl. 'Everybody knows how tough it is on kids to be in here for Christmas. And on their parents,' she added kindly. 'In fact, it's probably tougher on you than it is on your baby.'

It would have to be a baby she was in with, wouldn't it? She was so young.

'Tell me about it.' The girl was fishing in her bag again. This time it was for lip gloss. 'We've got the loveliest doctor, though. How 'bout you?'

Did she mean Andy? Was this the mother of his latest admission? And she was in here, trying to make herself look as attractive as possible?

Was that why *she* was beginning to feel judgmental? That there was something about this young woman she really didn't like?

'We're doing fine,' she said coolly, already moving away. 'We'll be going home tomorrow.'

'Lucky you. We'll probably be here for ages. Oh…damn…' A careless nudge as she leaned closer to the mirror had dislodged the bag and sent it flying to the floor. A heap of objects escaped to scatter themselves on the floor.

A small bottle rolled rapidly enough to knock Gemma's foot. She bent down and picked it up to hand it back but all those years of medical training made her glance automatically at the label as she did so.

A well-known brand of laxatives. Well…that might go some way to explaining why this girl was so thin. The bottle was snatched out of her hand with a haste that suggested Gemma was correct in thinking the medication might be being abused.

'Gotta run,' the girl said. 'Catch ya later.'

There wasn't much Andy could do for the three-year-old girl who'd been readmitted tonight, of all nights. The morphine she'd been given for the severe abdominal pain had worked its magic and the child was now comfortably asleep. A new raft of investigations would need to be ordered but that was a task for the morning and most of those tests would have to wait in any case. Only absolute emergencies could be dealt with on Christmas Day.

With some relief, Andy headed back to his office. Would Gemma still be there?

He hoped so.

Or did he? He'd been on the point of confessing how empty his life was without her. Feeling closer to her with every passing minute.

Would the barriers be back in place by now?

Gemma wasn't sitting in the armchair. She was standing beside his desk, staring at that photograph. She jumped when she heard him approach and when her gaze met his, she looked…guilty.

What for?

Nosing around in personal things or because the photograph reminded her of what they'd once had? What she'd thrown away?

Andy's breath came out in a sigh. Yes…the barriers were there again.

'How's it going?' he asked. 'That coffee was probably undrinkable.'

'I forgot about it. I went to check on the children.'

'They OK?'

'Sound asleep.'

'That's good. They'll be fine in the morning and ready to enjoy their Christmas Day.'

'I hope so.' Gemma was biting her bottom lip, a sure sign that she wasn't feeling comfortable. 'How's your patient?'

'Also asleep.' Andy shook his head. 'I have to confess I have no idea what's going on there.

We've done a raft of tests, including a CT, and everything's normal. Her mother's convinced she's got appendicitis. Wanted me to call in a surgeon immediately. She said she had her appendix out a couple of years ago and she reckons Chantelle's got exactly the same symptoms. Plus, she looked it up on the internet.'

'Oh...' Gemma's lips had an amused curve to them. 'Can't argue with the internet, can you?'

Andy smiled. 'Not easily, no.'

Gemma was watching him. The guilty expression had long since vanished. Right now she was looking as if she was concentrating hard on something.

'Chantelle's mother,' she said. 'Does she look about nineteen, long dark hair and a ton of jewellery?'

'That's her. Why?'

'I met her in the bathroom.'

Andy nodded. 'Yeah...she dashed off to the loo when I was examining Chantelle.'

'Does she...I mean...does something strike you as being a bit off key with her?'

Andy frowned. 'She's very young. Needs more reassurance than Chantelle, that's for sure.'

'Hmm.'

The sound that Gemma made took Andy back through the years. Right back to when they had both been junior doctors, in fact, and had spent hours discussing their cases and bouncing ideas around. Sparking off each other like that had been something they'd both loved. It had invariably pushed them both to think harder and perform better. And he recognised that sound. Gemma had thought of something he probably hadn't. The old response came automatically to his lips.

'OK, Einstein. Spill.'

Gemma's lips twitched but then her face became serious. 'Has Munchausen's by proxy occurred to you?'

Andy blinked. 'No. Should it?'

'Difficulty coming up with any kind of definitive diagnosis? A caregiver who's had the same symptoms as the child within the previous five years?'

'Mmm. It's not a conclusion I'd be happy jumping to.' He stared at Gemma, narrowing his eyes. 'You sound a bit too sure of yourself. Did Deidre say something in the bathroom?'

'No. It was more what she wasn't saying.'

'What do you mean?'

'She was busy fixing her make-up. Saying how awful it was to be stuck in hospital. Only she didn't sound that cut up about it, you know? And she didn't even mention her baby. And...'

'And?'

'And it might be nothing but she knocked her bag over and I picked up a bottle of pills. Laxatives.'

Andy could almost hear the penny dropping. 'Oh, hell,' he groaned. 'That would do it. Diarrhoea. Violent abdominal cramps. Normal test results.' He ran his hands through his hair, wondering how he was going to deal with this.

'Have you got access to Chantelle's previous health records?'

'Not yet. She only came in the first time a couple of days ago and they've moved recently from up north. We've requested information but…well, it is Christmas. Silly season.'

'Might be worth having a chat to someone. Maybe looking at the mother's records, too. It's another sign, isn't it? Moving around and going to new hospitals or doctors.'

Andy nodded. 'No time like the present. If I get any red flags, I could at least talk to Deirdre about it. Get those laxatives off her before she makes the poor kid suffer any more, if that is what's happening.'

He caught Gemma's gaze. They were both confident they were on the right track. They both knew that if they *were* right, mother and child would need a lot of help and it would be far better to step in now before any real harm was done.

'I'll come and find you,' Andy said. 'And let you know what they say.'

It was over an hour later when Andy eased open the door of the children's room. Gemma had been dozing in the armchair but came awake instantly when she'd sensed the movement.

The only light came from the nightlights plugged in low to the floor in both the room and the corridor outside, but Gemma could see how tense Andy was.

Or maybe it was more that she could sense it. The same way she'd picked up the silent opening of the door when she'd been more than half-asleep.

Gemma uncurled her legs and got to her feet. As she got closer to Andy she could see how still he was holding himself. How wary the expression in his eyes was. He wasn't at all sure he wanted to be here, was he? The tension felt like nervousness. Borderline fear, even?

It was instantly contagious. They'd always been able to connect effortlessly. To gauge and respond to each other on both intellectual and emotional levels.

Andy was here because something had changed. He wanted—or needed—time with *her*. A heartbeat later, his words confirmed the impression.

'I need some fresh air,' Andy muttered quietly. 'Want to come with me?'

Did she?

Gemma could feel her heart rate accelerating. Her mouth felt dry. A short time ago, in his office, she had sensed them getting closer and had been so disappointed when Andy had pushed her away with the impersonal questions about her life in Sydney.

The opposite was happening here.

And that was making Gemma feel very, very nervous.

It was Christmas Eve, for heaven's sake. A time of year that bound them together with memories that were very painful. It could be the worst time to try and reconnect on a deeper level.

Or…it might be the only time when emotions could be strong enough to break down barriers.

Andy was holding out his hand and suddenly Gemma had her answer.

Of course she wanted to go with him. She *had* to.

No words were needed on her part. Gemma simply put her hand in Andy's.

He led them at a fast pace along the corridor, out of the ward and up a stairwell.

'Don't worry. I've told Lisa to page me if any of the children wake up.'

Up and up the stairs they went until they came to a heavy metal fire door. Gemma knew exactly where they were going. It was the place they'd often headed for as young doctors, when the only time they'd seemed to get alone together had been moments they'd been able to escape from work and come here.

On to the roof of Queen Mary Infirmary.

The air was fresh all right.

Freezing, in fact, but Gemma wasn't about to complain. It wasn't bothering her yet because she was so aware of the warmth of Andy's hand.

He was still holding it. Up all those stairs and even when he'd pushed open the heavy door to the roof space. Now, as the blast of icy air hit, he increased the pressure of his grip.

'Can you stand it?'

Gemma could only nod. Oh…yes…

'It's pretty cold,' Andy added as he led them

on a route that had once been so well trodden. Round the back of the structure that held the workings of the nearest set of lifts. Into a sheltered corner well away from the heli-pad. A private place that had a great view over the city of Manchester. The blinking light of a plane coming in to land could be seen beneath the heavy, low-slung clouds.

'Santa's sleigh, you reckon?' Gemma smiled but couldn't repress a small shiver.

Andy didn't smile at her weak joke. 'I just need a minute,' he apologised. 'Head-clearing stuff. The cold is...cleansing or something, I guess.'

'Oh...' Gemma understood instantly. 'We were right, then.'

'*You* were.' But something made Andy pause and take a slow, inward breath.

'We' was more accurate. He'd been reminded at the time of the way they'd once sparked off each other professionally and come up with things that had been more than the sum of different ideas. Something that had pushed them both into being better doctors. Better people even?

It had been the same as parenting together.

The same as making love.

They had always been a perfect team. Two halves of a whole that was impossible to achieve alone. Or with anybody else.

God…how could he have forgotten how powerful that was? How much…*less* his life was without it?

Feeling it again now was terrifying. How the hell was he going to say goodbye to her tomorrow and watch her walk out of his life again?

Andy cleared his throat and deliberately avoided catching Gemma's gaze. Avoided saying anything remotely personal. The only thing he couldn't bring himself to do was break the handclasp. He needed that touch. That warmth. To feel that connection for just a little longer.

'First hospital I rang where she was last living was able to fill me in. Mind you, it wouldn't have mattered what hospital I rang. She's well known in the system up there. Had a perfectly normal appendix removed the year before she had a baby and someone finally flagged the possibility of Munchausen's.

'Maybe that procedure was major enough to keep her happy for a while. Or maybe becoming a mother changed something. This is the first time Chantelle's been the patient instead of Deirdre.'

'Thank goodness it's been caught early. I've heard of cases that went on for years and years before the truth came out.'

'Mmm. This could have gone the same way if I didn't have so much faith in your instincts. She denied it all fiercely at first. Until I called her bluff and said there was an easy blood test I could do to check for something like laxatives in Chantelle's blood and then she knew she was busted and it all came out along with a lot of tears.'

Gemma squeezed his hand. It would have been an emotional and difficult conversation to have had. And he still had faith in her instincts? For some reason, it felt like a much bigger compliment than telling her she had never needed to wear mascara. It felt like the way they'd once been together. A perfect team.

'I've referred her to the psych team and Social Services will be notified tomorrow.' Andy stopped talking and heaved a sigh as he closed his eyes. 'It wasn't pleasant. We do everything we can to keep parents and their kids together. Goes against the grain to start something that might break them up.'

He opened his eyes and looked straight at Gemma.

'Enough about me. You OK, Gem?'

His tone was so gentle. So caring. His face got a bit blurry as tears stung her eyes.

'He's always there, isn't he?' Andy went on in that same, soft voice. 'When you hear a baby cry in the distance. Or when you have to deal with someone who has a kid and they don't know how lucky they are.'

Gemma nodded. Yes. The memories of Max were always there.

'It doesn't hurt so much these days, though, does it?'

Gemma shook her head. It was true. Time might not heal things like that completely but the pain was…encapsulated somehow now.

'I find I can remember the good bits now and it doesn't automatically undo me,' Andy said. 'Do you?'

Gemma nodded again. Her voice seemed to have deserted her. Because she was afraid that by speaking she might break the spell that Andy's words were casting?

'Is there one thing that stands out for you?' Andy's question was gentle. She didn't have to go there if she didn't want to. 'A favourite memory?'

Gemma didn't have to take any time to think about the answer to that question.

'Holding him that first time,' she whispered. 'Feeling like…a mother.'

It wasn't the whole answer. Or the whole memory. Because a huge part of what had created the magic of that moment had been seeing Andy's big hands cradling his newborn son with such exquisitely gentle care and reverence. The way she had felt overwhelmed with love.

For both Andy and Max.

Andy was nodding. It felt like he was stroking the top of her head. 'For me, too. That extraordinary feeling of being more than a couple. Being…a family. Nothing prepares you for how different it feels. And you'd never really know if you hadn't been there yourself, would you?'

Gemma swallowed. Hard. 'No.'

Andy had harnessed that knowledge. Used it to become the kind of doctor who could relate to children and their parents. She had no doubt that his caring extended to the whole family of any of his young patients. It was far more than she had been brave enough to do.

His words were making her remember more than the magic of a new family being created. They had taken her back to older memories. To when they *were* just a couple. To when that had seemed too good to be improved on.

She needed to say something else. To try and move the conversation on. Could she do it without breaking the spell that seemed to have caught them both?

'The first time Max smiled,' she offered softly. 'That's a special memory. He...he looked so like you.'

A miniature version of the smile she loved so much. Had loved since the first time she'd seen it. When she'd been standing outside the door of little Jessica's room in the PICU, too scared to go inside and begin what she knew she had to do. When he'd offered to be her support person and he'd smiled in a way that made her feel more courageous all by itself. Not alone any more. Brave enough to cope with anything.

'I still remember how jealous I was when he spoke his first words. You remember what they were?'

Of course she did.

'Mum, mum, mum.'

Gemma's indrawn breath was a gulp. At the same moment her body decided to let her know how cold it really was out here by shuddering dramatically.

'Oh...Gem...' Andy pulled her close.

Gemma could feel herself snuggling closer to

Andy and she didn't feel cold any more. How could she with his arms around her like this? So close she could feel the steady thump of his heart?

For a long moment they stood there in silence. Gemma could feel when Andy's head tipped so that his cheek was resting on the top of her head. It felt so familiar. So good.

As if she'd come home after far too long away.

'I'm so sorry.' Andy's voice was a rumble against her ear. 'I didn't mean to stir it all up again...'

'It's...OK...' Gemma sniffed and took a deep breath as she raised her face from the warmth and comfort of Andy's chest. 'Really,' she added, seeing the concern on his face. 'It's part of my life and I couldn't forget Max even if I wanted to. Which I don't. Ever. And...if I try and share those memories with anyone else, they...'

'They don't share them,' Andy continued for her. 'They can't possibly understand.'

No. The only people in the world who could

still share Max were his parents. His mother and father. Andy and herself.

There was no way she could break the eye contact. It was intense and it held shared memories that were deeper than the 'snapshot' moments they'd had with their baby.

They were the memories of how much of a team they'd been. Andy had been the husband that most women would dream of. Rarely complaining about having to take his turn cooking or doing dishes. Happy to do the supermarket run and put the rubbish out and even clean the loo. They might have both felt they were doing more than their share at times but that's what it had taken to be young parents together so they had done it. Together. And it would have been enough if Max hadn't got sick.

It hadn't just been sharing all those household duties. They had both worked irregular and long hours, slotting in extra study when they'd been able to, juggling the days and nights so that Max would have one parent with him for as much time as was humanly possible.

Gemma remembered Andy bringing her a cup of coffee at some horribly early hour after they'd both been up half the night with a teething baby. She remembered him sitting on the side of her bed, stroking her hair until she woke up enough to drink it and then get ready for a day at work. She remembered the guilt she'd felt, knowing that Andy would probably get no sleep during the day and would then have to front up for a night shift and he'd make damn sure he was awake enough to do his job well.

Had she really secretly blamed him for falling asleep for so long on the day that Max died?

Oh…God…

Still the eye contact went on. She could see that a million thoughts were racing through Andy's mind as well.

Was he thinking the same thing? That, once, they had been such a great team? An amazing little family?

How could she have walked away from that?

Gemma's lips trembled. She willed herself not to cry but it was hard.

She had hurt them both so badly. The kind of hurt that could never be undone or even repaired. She had destroyed everything they'd tried to cling to in the wake of losing their child.

They couldn't go back.

Except…the way Andy was *looking* at her now…

It made Gemma think that some things hadn't changed at all. They'd been covered up, yes, but the love that had brought them together all those years ago was still there.

Was it possible she could ask Andy to forgive her?

Gemma's eyes had always been the most astonishing Andy had ever seen. It had been the colour that had struck him first, of course. Those gold flecks and the perfect, matching halos around the edge of the irises. But it hadn't taken very long to get caught by so much more.

They said that the eyes were the windows to the soul and, sure, Gemma had stained-glass beauties instead of plain glass but it was the light

that shone through that made them so extraordinarily beautiful as far as he was concerned.

She'd asked him for some spare courage in
that first exchange of words but he'd known she
hadn't really needed it. The more he'd learned
about her the more he'd realised how right he'd
been.

Gemma had been courageous her entire life.
She'd been a protector and mother figure for her
baby sister. She'd fought for the chance to use
her intelligence and perseverance to succeed in
her dream career. She'd stepped up to the plate
when she'd been faced with an unexpected pregnancy and she had loved Max as much as he had.

She still hurt, as much as he did. He could see
it in her eyes now.

He couldn't look away. Because he could see
more than the pain of the poignant memories
they shared.

He could see the connection they'd always had.
The love?

Was it possible that Gemma…? The thought
dissolved as the emotional response to what he

could see tipped Andy into a place he hadn't been in for many, many years.

A place where passion ruled and everything else in the world ceased to exist.

The only muscles that moved in his body were the tiny ones that controlled his eyes but he felt them as his gaze finally left Gemma's and dropped to her mouth.

Maybe it was the trembling of her lips that tipped him over the edge of control. He was holding the woman he'd loved so much in his arms. He could feel the shape of her. The warmth of her body despite the sub-zero temperatures. His own heart was speeding up to match the thump of her pulse against his chest.

What man could have resisted that tremble? He needed to make it go away so that Gemma wouldn't be so unhappy. His hands were already in use, holding her against him, so the only part of his body that he had available was his mouth. Without thinking, Andy lowered his head and covered her lips with his own.

A light touch. Meant to be comforting. Broken almost as soon as it was made.

But then Andy raised his gaze to her eyes again.

And the world stopped.

They were both in that space now. Nothing else existed. It was just the two of them and the pull between them was a force that was overwhelming.

This time Gemma moved at the same time Andy did. Their mouths met with a pressure that was almost painful. Andy had to let go of Gemma's body and cradle her head to protect it, but he still felt the thump as her back came up against the wall. He felt her hands gripping his arms and then sliding up, touching the sides of his face before her fingers were buried in his hair.

It wasn't enough. It didn't matter how many times he changed the angle of the kiss or how hard he pressed or how often his tongue danced with Gemma's.

It just wasn't enough.

Maybe nothing could be.

They were both completely out of breath when

they finally pulled apart. They stood there, shocked at what had just happened.

The evidence of the passion that they still shared.

As if driven by shared frustration, they both moved again but this time they both jerked back the instant before their lips touched.

There was confusion mixed with desire now.

Should they be giving in to this?

Could they go far enough to satisfy that desire?

And, if they did, would there be any point given that the way they'd parted had destroyed any possibility of a future relationship because a relationship had to be built on trust? It wasn't that he wouldn't *want* to trust her again. He just *couldn't*. That self-protection mechanism was too strong.

Andy could feel his physical response to Gemma closing down. Getting locked away. When their eye contact broke, they both moved apart. Turned away from each other.

What had just happened there?

Gemma barely heard Andy mutter something

about needing to get back inside before they both froze to death.

Whatever it was that had just happened, it was over.

But there was no denying that it *had* happened. Dear Lord... She didn't even know whether Andy was single any more. Maybe he wasn't and that was why he'd pulled down the shutters and turned away.

Had it just been a response to being so close? Sharing memories that were theirs alone?

A blast from the past?

Andy wasn't even touching her now. There would be no hand-holding on the way back to the ward. He wasn't looking at her either as he held open the fire door for her to go back inside. He was staring up at the night sky.

'Santa's sleigh seems to be caught in a holding pattern,' he said. 'Let's hope he gets to land before morning.'

Gemma's quick smile was automatic but she said nothing.

Her brain was too busy thinking about something very different.

Another Christmas. The last one they had shared. The final blow to their marriage that was now the barrier that could keep them apart for ever.

The year they'd lost Max had been the ultimate Christmas from hell. But that last one hadn't been so far behind, had it?

CHAPTER NINE

Christmas: four years ago

'SO YOU'RE not working on Christmas Day this year, then?'

'No.' Gemma was glad the room she was in was too dark for her consultant to read the expression on her face. She knew it would be one of utter dread.

'Got family stuff on?'

'Mmm.' The oppressive weight of that dread intensified. She had known it would be like this. Why…oh, *why* had she let Laura bully her into it?

'Please, Gemma. I want this to be a real Christmas. A family one. You and Andy can't go through the rest of your lives avoiding every celebration that involves kids. It's not fair. On me or Ev or the children…' She'd been crying by now. *'Most of all it's not fair on you. You've got to start…*

I don't know…living again. Not just working. I know how hard it is but…please, Gem. Just try? Ev's already talked to Andy and he said he'll come. Please…'

The radiology consultant cleared his throat. 'Anyway…let's get this tutorial out of the way, shall we? Tell me about case nine.'

The only source of light in this room was coming from the glass screens that had X-ray images clipped onto them.

'There's a focal shadow in the right lower lobe. Suggestive of pneumonia.'

'Differential diagnoses?'

'Carcinoma and lymphoma.'

'Good. Case ten?'

Gemma didn't have to look at the image for more than a few seconds. 'Classic evidence of left ventricular failure.'

'Such as?'

'Cardiomegaly, upper lobe and pulmonary vein diversion and…' Gemma had to grin. 'I can see sternotomy wires so it's highly likely this patient has had coronary bypass surgery.'

The older man chuckled. 'I don't think I've got anything in this lot that's going to trip you up. You pass, Gemma. Tutorials are over. You're perfectly competent in X-ray interpretation and you know when you need to call in a second opinion. Now...you going to come to the departmental Christmas party after work today?'

'No.'

There was a tiny silence in the dark. 'Nobody would ever call you a party animal, Gemma, but couldn't you make an exception just this once?'

Oh...great... There seemed to be a conspiracy going on, courtesy of the festive season. Did everybody see it as the perfect time to give her a bit of a push? Propel her back into the land of the living and the happy? Make everything all right again?

Fix things between Andy and herself even?

Gemma let her breath out in a long sigh. She hadn't even seen Andy that morning because he'd got up well before her. She'd known there was something he wanted to say to her because she'd sensed him standing there at the bedroom door, looking at her.

And she'd pretended to be still deeply asleep.

He'd simply let himself quietly out of the apartment without saying goodbye. Without even pausing long enough to have breakfast.

She would have to go and see him now. She'd been putting it off all day, letting her job fill her head. Telling herself she was too busy to think about anything else. Too busy to even answer when he'd texted her. Three times.

Staying inside her comfort zone. Not thinking about her reluctant agreement to visit Andy on the paediatric ward before she went home. A concession that had been dragged out of her at the end of their last, awful argument.

'It's where I work, Gem. Everybody's partners come to the Christmas party. I'm not even asking you to come to that, but, for God's sake, couldn't you just show your face on the ward? The staff up there think my wife is just a figment of my imagination. Sometimes it feels that way to me, too.'

'You know what they say…' The radiology consultant was on his feet, flicking off the X-ray screens. Any moment now he would turn on the main light and Gemma would have to be careful what showed on her face. 'All work and no play...'

'Yeah...yeah...' Gemma smiled to keep her tone light. 'The paper I want to get finished is interesting enough to count as play. I've got all the stats. I just need to write up the discussion bit.'

'The one about the false negatives in head injury with CT scans read by ED staff?'

'That's the one.'

'Sounds like work to me.'

Gemma shrugged. All work and no play was fine by her. It was pretty much what had kept her sane for the last two years.

Had her permit for staying in that safe place run out? Was that why she was aware of the increasing pressure to start behaving differently?

Was there more to Laura's passionate plea for a family Christmas than met the eye? When had Evan talked to Andy about it? Maybe he'd had a heart-to-heart with Laura as well. Maybe they'd all decided that if she could be surrounded by children and happy times she might decide that she was ready to try again.

The sensation of dread was suffocating now. Was that what Andy wanted to talk to her about?

Having another baby?

No. She wasn't going there. She couldn't. She couldn't even bring herself to talk about it.

'Well…have a great Christmas anyway.' The consultant was heading home. 'See you in the new year.'

'You, too.' Gemma could feel how tight her smile was. Every cell in her body seemed to be holding itself rigid.

Of course there was a conspiracy. Laura was pregnant again, wasn't she? And it wasn't enough to highlight the lack in Gemma and Andy's lives by simply having another baby. This time she was pregnant with *twins*.

The pressure was building. Something was going to snap and Gemma knew it was going to hurt someone. Herself? Of course. But what about the other people in her life?

Laura and Evan.

Cute three-year-old Hazel and her baby brother, Jamie.

Andy…

And hadn't she already hurt Andy enough?

Oh, yes…more than enough.

It was probably the understatement of the century that she hadn't been easy to live with for the past two years. She'd been perfectly well aware of how much it had hurt Andy to be shut out but she hadn't been capable of engaging with anyone on more than a professional level. The rest of her had become numb within days of losing Max. In the beginning she'd been grateful for that numbness. Clung to it, in fact, when anything threatened to penetrate. And then, when she'd been ready to try and feel again, she hadn't known how and that had been frightening. It had been so much easier to retreat back into the safe, numb space.

But the safety barriers of that comfort zone seemed to be crumbling and, yes, it was because it was Christmas. She'd been given a free pass to avoid all the emotional connotations last year but nothing came without a price tag eventually, did it?

She was going to have to pay this time.

And Gemma knew she was going to be dipping into an account that was still overdrawn.

'Hey, Dr Andy. D'ya know what day it is tomorrow?'

'Sure do, John Boy.' Andy dropped to a couch to put him at eye level with the seven-year-old boy he'd come to know very well during his time as a paediatric registrar. 'It's Christmas.'

John Boy's smile was enough to make you think that life was wonderful. This admission had been to try and correct a badly deformed bone in his lower leg to preserve his ability to walk a little longer. He had a complicated external fixation device from knee to ankle but he was up on crutches already and into mischief all over the ward. He got away with all sorts of things, from small misdemeanours like raiding the fridge in the staffroom to major naughtiness like going

AWOL from the ward and ending up somewhere like the hospital laundry. It wasn't just because he'd spent his short life either in hospital or foster-care. It was because of that smile.

The one that said that, yes, life was full of hard stuff but you could find good stuff, too, and if you didn't make the most of it, you were pretty stupid.

It was being around kids like John Boy that had given Andy a way forward in life.

If only Gemma could meet him. Or any of the other children that came through these doors on a regular basis. Or their families, who managed to stick together during the hard times and gain strength from each other.

'I'm gonna get presents.' John Boy's smile was still lighting up his small, dark face. 'I always do when I'm in here for Christmas. Santa comes.'

'I heard that.' More than heard it. He was lined up to don the costume and do it himself this year. He'd have to disguise his voice when he was handing out the gifts to the children. John Boy was probably too smart to get fooled for a moment but he'd probably go along with the pretence simply because it was fun. Andy hoped the gifts with this boy's name on them were special ones this year because he gave so much to others without even realising it.

'I'm gonna tell that new kid that came in today. He was crying.'

'Paul? He's not feeling so good today, John Boy. Why don't you just say hi and give him a smile?'

'Okey-dokey.' John Boy concentrated hard and moved his crutches. The short conversation had been enough to make him breathless so he waited for a moment before pushing his body into motion. 'See ya, Dr Andy.'

'See ya, John Boy.'

Andy watched the lad's slow movement down the corridor. He saw a nurse spot John Boy and smile as if her day had just brightened out of sight. He wished Gemma was here. If only she could receive that gift of knowing how good life could still be in the face of the difficult stuff. But how could she receive anything emotional like that when she'd shut herself off so completely?

Andy was at his wits' end. He'd tried everything he could think of. At first it had been easy to know what to do because they had both been so shattered by their grief. All they had been able to do had been to hold onto each other and cry.

He'd reached a point, after a few months of that desperately sad place, where he'd had to move forward to save himself. Gemma had agreed that it was the right thing to do but had simply refused to come with him. Worse than that. She had moved in the opposite direction. Andy had faced the tough stuff head on. It was hard to be around children and he couldn't let it grow into something that would destroy too much of him so he'd chosen paediatrics for his specialty.

Gemma had chosen not only to avoid children but to avoid people as much as she could. She'd chosen radiology as a specialty and spent most of her working life shut into a dark room, analysing the images that the technicians obtained from patients.

She'd hurled herself into postgraduate study as well so that when they were home together she was invariably on the computer or buried in a textbook. The care they had taken of each other in the early days after that dreadful Christmas had morphed into a relationship that felt like housemates. Polite housemates who had sex occasionally, sure, but something huge was missing. And it was something that had been there before they'd had Max so his absence from their lives wasn't enough to explain that massive hole.

Trying to push at all only led to fights but Andy was getting desperate. So was Laura.

'We've got to do something, Andy. I think she's lost and if we don't reach out and grab her, she'll disappear for ever. It's Christmas. The perfect time. Maybe the last chance we'll get.'

An hour or two with her sister's family for Christmas dinner wasn't going to be enough for Andy, however. He was desperate to get their professional lives to connect again, too. So he'd pushed and forced her to agree to come to the paediatric departmental party today.

And then he'd had second thoughts that morning when he'd stood there, watching her sleep.

Feeling the gulf between them but knowing how much he still loved her. Wondering if she really *was* asleep or just avoiding him…again. He'd tried texting her a few times today, too. He just wanted to talk. If it was too much for her, she didn't have to go to the stupid party. They could go somewhere by themselves. Maybe, if he could show her that he was trying to understand, at least it could open the door to some real communication.

'You still here, Andy? Thought you'd be at the party by now.'

'I'll head off soon.' He'd give Gemma another ten minutes and if she hadn't arrived by then he'd go past Radiology and see if she was still at work. She'd said she'd text him but maybe things were really busy. Perhaps that was why she hadn't answered any of his messages. Why she hadn't turned up to visit his ward.

He used the ten minutes to wander around, seeing what everybody was up to. A Christmas movie was playing in the dayroom for the children who were well enough to be out of bed. A nurse who had angel wings pinned to the back of her uniform and a tinsel halo on her head was handing out ice-block treats. John Boy was using his like a sword to play with another small boy in a wheelchair. The Christmas tree had its lights flashing and there were spraypainted snowflakes on the windows.

A nurse was holding the door of a storage area open for a man Andy recognised as a patient's father. He grinned and took an armload of carrier bags into the private space. The nurse picked up one of the rolls of Christmas wrapping paper he'd dropped and handed it in before closing the door. She grinned at Andy, putting her finger to her lips.

Christmas carols were playing at the nurses' station and being sung along to with varying degrees of tunefulness. A tired-looking mother paused to listen and miraculously the crying baby in her arms became quiet. Her companion, probably her husband, was holding a toddler on his hip. The two parents exchanged a smile of pure relief as the baby settled.

Andy smiled, too.

And then he turned and his smile faded. Gemma was standing there, staring at the couple. At the baby the woman was holding?

No. It was the toddler that had caught her attention. Less than two years old, the little boy was wearing a Santa hat. Like Max had been in that last photograph of him that had ever been taken.

Oh…help.

'Gemma.' Andy pasted his smile back in place. 'I was just coming to find you.'

He could see how carefully she was holding herself. When he put his arm around her shoulders, he could feel a tension that made his heart plummet. She felt brittle enough to snap at any moment. She'd kept her promise but right now Andy wished she hadn't. It had been a bad idea to push her into this.

'You know what?' He began leading her out of the ward. 'I don't think I want to hang around here any longer today. Let me grab my jacket and we could head out for a drink. Dinner, maybe.'

'I…I'd rather just go home. I want to finish

that paper I'm writing up for *Radiology Today*.'
Gemma was walking just slightly ahead of Andy,
taking her shoulders out of range for his arm. She
was talking quickly. Sounding too bright. 'You
know, the one about the false negatives for CT
interpretation by ED staff?'

She was running again, Andy thought sadly.
Avoiding anything that could be deemed too personal. Anything that required an emotional response.

He couldn't live like this any longer. He knew
the Gemma he loved was still there somewhere
but he was too bone tired of trying to coax her
back.

'It's almost Christmas,' he said. 'It's time to
stop thinking about work for a few days.' Taking a longer step, he got close enough to put his
hand on Gemma's shoulder. 'It's the time people
like to be with the people they care about. That's
all I'm asking for…a bit of time with you. Is that
too much to ask?'

'Of course not. Sorry.' Gemma's pace slowed.
'It's just…' She stopped and turned, looking up at

him. 'It's Christmas, Andy. I can't...' She caught her bottom lip between her teeth. 'It's too...soon.'

The pain in her eyes cut into Andy. A rare glimpse of the real Gemma. But how long could he keep comforting her? Telling her that things would come right in time and that she would find a way through this? She thought she'd found the answer in burying herself in her career but she was so wrong. Not that he could suggest anything else. He'd tried to get her to go to professional counselling. He'd even once suggested that she might need antidepressant medication and that had led to a row that had lasted for weeks. She could cope, she'd yelled at him, but only if she was allowed to cope in her own way.

'Just leave me alone. Why can't you leave me the hell alone?'

Laura could be right. Gemma was lost and something had to be done.

'It's been two years, Gem,' he said quietly. 'We *have* to move on.'

Her eyes widened with shock. '*We* have to move

on? You did that a long time ago, Andy. This isn't *your* problem.'

'What do you mean?' They weren't far away from the office Andy shared with the other departmental registrars. He walked to the door and opened it, then turned and stared at Gemma.

This was it. They couldn't shove it all under the carpet any more. They had to confront this issue before it destroyed them, no matter how painful that might be.

Andy looked so *angry*.

Or was that desperate?

Gemma couldn't find any of that comforting numbness to pull around her as she forced her feet to move and take her into the office. She knew she couldn't brush this off by dismissing the conversation because she had something really important that had to be done. Like writing some totally irrelevant professional article.

This was what was important.

Their relationship.

Their future.

She was being dragged out of whatever safe place she had managed to create for herself, whether she was ready or not.

Because Andy couldn't wait any longer.

And fair enough.

Two years? It really had been that long, hadn't it? Nothing like having an anniversary that coincided with something like Christmas to make sure you could never forget.

Gemma stopped as soon as Andy closed the office door behind her. The other registrars were not here. They were probably at the staff Christmas party. Someone had strung tinsel around the room and there was a miniature fir tree on one of the desks, decorated with boiled sweets tied to the branches. A gift from a patient? Christmas cards, some home-made, with children's drawings were pinned to the notice-board.

The room was small but Andy put as much distance between them as he could before turning to face her.

That hurt.

Were things really so bad that he didn't even want to be within touching distance right now?

'I don't know what to do, Gemma.' Andy's voice was low. And raw. 'I've been careful not to try and push you. I've given you all the support and space I know how to give. So has Laura. And Evan. We've *all* done everything we could to help you get through losing Max. You've got the career you always wanted but...' He pushed both his hands through his hair, making it stand up in spikes before holding his hands up in a gesture of surrender.

'But it's *all* you seem to want now. Your career. You don't have time for me. Or for your family. You won't have anything to do with children if you can help it. You won't even have anything to do with Christmas. And Christmas comes around every year, Gemma.' Andy's voice was getting louder.

'Whether you're ready for it or not, it comes and you have to *deal* with it. You can't hide for ever.'

'I'm not hiding. I said I'd go to Laura's this

year. I've...I've got presents for the kids. I'm *trying*, Andy.'

'You've refused to go to any Christmas parties here. You flat out refused to have a single decoration at home, let alone a Christmas tree.'

'You can't turn around without bumping into a Christmas tree around here.' Gemma waved her hand at the small version on the desk to emphasise her point. 'We don't *need* one at home.'

'I think we do.' Andy's voice was so controlled now. So vehement. Gemma had never heard him sound like this and it frightened her. 'I think it would be a symbol. That we've got past a tragedy. That we've still got some kind of future.'

Oh...God... Was this an ultimatum?

Andy was rubbing his forehead now. Clearly, he was finding this difficult but he couldn't stop. Something had been unleashed that couldn't be caught and locked away again. When he looked back at Gemma, his face was anguished.

'I just don't understand,' he said. 'Why can't you get past it? You never even wanted a baby in the first place.'

Something cold trickled down Gemma's spine. She couldn't deny that, could she? She couldn't say that things had changed the moment she'd held Max in her arms for the first time or that being a family had meant as much to her as it did to Andy.

She hadn't wanted to be pregnant. She'd wanted her career. To outward appearances, she had spent the last two years simply proving that. Looking as though she was relieved not to have the constraints of being a mother holding her back. Spending every waking hour working.

She'd thought Andy had understood that it was the only way she'd been able to get through each day. He'd done the same thing, hadn't he? Thrown himself into his work? He'd tried to be interested in the specialty she'd chosen but she hadn't been able to return that interest. Why hadn't she seen just how far it was pushing them apart?

Maybe she had but she'd put off trying to do anything about it because it was too hard. Too painful.

This was too painful. He was reminding her of

something she'd felt ashamed of even thinking after Max's birth.

It reminded her of something else that had haunted her ever since.

'And you only married me because I was pregnant.'

A stunned silence fell. Andy looked as though she'd given him a physical blow. As though he had to stay very still for a moment to work out exactly where he'd been injured. When he spoke again, his voice was soft. Almost defeated.

'So why am I still here, Gem? For God's sake… I *love* you. All I want is for you to be happy because it's becoming very obvious that nobody around you is going to be happy unless you are.'

'It's…harder for me.'

'What is?'

The numb place had vanished completely. Gemma felt like she had in those awful days before she'd discovered it. Her heart was breaking all over again.

'I…' I miss my baby, she wanted to cry. I miss holding him and hearing him laugh. I see his smile every time *you* smile. I feel so empty. Like there's nothing left…just a big, black hole…

The words wouldn't come out. Gemma was too scared to break the dam because she knew the flood would drown her.

'You think it's been *easy* for me?' Andy sounded incredulous. 'To get over losing our child?'

Gemma stared back at him helplessly. Of course he'd coped better than she had. 'You *work* with children,' she whispered.

'And you think it's been *easy*? That it doesn't remind me of Max and break my heart every time something goes wrong?' Gemma could see his Adam's apple bob as he swallowed hard.

'I love kids. I always have. The *easy* thing to do would have been to avoid them. Like you did. But I knew that would have ended up being only half a life so I took the hard road and jumped in the deep end. I didn't know whether I'd sink or swim but I did know that I understand how parents feel and that I'd do whatever it took to win the battle to save a child's life.'

Maybe that explained why Andy had gone off to work day after day, looking so grim. He'd had to find the strength to face his demons and he'd never told her because…because he'd been trying to protect her? Knowing she was facing her own demons in her own way? Oh…dear Lord…

'It's who I am now,' Andy continued. 'Who I'll be for the rest of my life.' His breath came out in a huff. 'Maybe it was meant to happen so that I would be this person. So I could spend my working life doing the best I can to keep families together. It doesn't mean I don't still want to have my *own* family. Can't you understand that?'

Gemma nodded, very slowly. Of course she could understand it. She'd always known that Andy wanted to have a family of his own. She'd watched the way he'd been drawn further into her sister's family over the last months. How much he loved being with Hazel and little Jamie. He didn't know about the twins yet but she could imagine the look on his face when he was given the news.

The longing she would see there.

She couldn't do it. She couldn't face being pregnant again and giving birth and holding an infant with the knowledge that it could all be ripped away. There wasn't enough of her heart left as it was. If any more got ripped out, it wouldn't be able to sustain life even.

Andy was walking towards her. He took her hands in his.

'I love you, Gem,' he said quietly.

'I…I love you, too,' she whispered.

'Then help me. Help *us*. We can't live like this for ever. It's been two years of hell. Isn't that long enough?'

Gemma could only nod. She had done this. Put Andy through months and months of hell because she hadn't been brave enough to even try putting her feet in the water, let alone jumping in at any deep end. This *was* all her fault. But she couldn't fix it, could she? Not if it meant having another baby.

Andy pulled her close and held her tightly. So tightly she couldn't breathe but that was OK. She didn't want to breathe because if she did, she'd have to think. And all she could think about was how she was destroying the person she loved most in the world.

'I need a drink,' she heard him say above her head. 'Come with me?'

Gemma shook her head this time. Somehow she found her voice and the words that might give her a brief reprieve.

'I think I need a bit of time on my own. To… think. Why don't you go to your Christmas party for a while and have a drink there?'

The pressure around her body eased a little too quickly. Andy knew he was being pushed away. He stepped back and Gemma knew he was watching her but she kept her head down. She couldn't face meeting his eyes just yet. Not with this new knowledge of how much she had failed their marriage. Would continue to fail it. After a long, silent moment Andy turned away and left, leaving only the echo of a sad sigh.

The apartment felt cold and empty.

Gemma couldn't stay there. Why on earth

hadn't they moved somewhere else after Max had died? Made a fresh start?

Because she hadn't suggested it? They'd all been tiptoeing around her. Trying to protect her. Letting her build her defensive walls and use her career like a statement of denial about how deeply she'd been hurt.

She couldn't deny anything now.

And she couldn't stay here.

Gemma had no idea what she should do. She knew Andy loved her. If she told him she could never face the prospect of having another baby, he would take that on board and live with it.

And it would always be there as an undercurrent in their marriage. A resentment that would simmer away in dark corners ready to explode if tension built from any cause.

It was blindingly simple really.

Andy wanted a family. She didn't. *Couldn't.*

And, because she loved Andy with all the heart she had left, she had to set him free to get what he wanted from his life.

It might destroy her but she was broken anyway, wasn't she? At least Andy had the guts to face life and put the pieces back together again. To *live*. All she was doing was surviving.

But the decision was too big. Too terrifying. Maybe what she needed to do was give them both some space so that, when they saw each other again, they could talk about it.

Yes. That was the first step. Gemma pulled a suitcase from the storeroom that had once been a nursery. Mechanically, she began opening drawers and pulling out items that she might need for a few days. Underwear and tights. Nightwear and jeans. She moved to the wardrobe and pulled things off random hangers without even thinking, rolling the items of clothing and stuffing them into the suitcase.

Where would she go?

The obvious answer was to Laura and Evan's house but how would that help? Laura was just as worried about her as Andy was. She would want to see their marriage survive and she would try and convince Gemma that another baby was exactly what was needed. Of course she would.

She was probably glowing with her own new pregnancy already.

And it was *Christmas*.

And Jamie was almost the same age as Max had been when…when…

Gemma almost couldn't see what she was stuffing into a toilet bag in the bathroom.

She was falling again.

Falling apart.

She couldn't go to Laura's. She'd leave the gifts for Andy to take. She would text Laura to say she was sorry but she needed some time on her own and then she'd turn her phone off so she couldn't receive a response.

She couldn't stay here.

She could go to a hotel but that wouldn't be far enough. If she was within reach of Andy she could never do what she had to do.

Set him free. Give him a 'get out of hell' card.

He could find someone else. Someone who would be able to be the mother to the children he wanted.

Could she stand seeing that happen? No. Even

being in another city in England would be too close. She had to get further away. Maybe as far as the other side of the world?

Where was her passport?

It took some hunting down. It was in a desk drawer, along with all sorts of other bits and pieces. Lanyards with name tags from various conferences she and Andy had attended over the last couple of years. Some keys, the usefulness of which had been long forgotten. An old phone charger. Paper clips and even bits of rubbish.

No.

Gemma stared at the item in her hand. It wasn't rubbish exactly but why had this been shoved in a drawer and not thrown out when it had last been seen two years ago?

It was that piece of plastic mistletoe.

It was also the final straw because Gemma couldn't even remember when Andy had last kissed her.

She dropped the piece of mistletoe and picked up her passport. And her suitcase.

And left.

CHAPTER TEN

IT WAS almost dawn.

Christmas Day.

Gemma hadn't seen Andy since she'd followed him down from the roof of the Queen Mary Infirmary.

'I have to duck home for a bit. I need to collect the Santa suit I'll be wearing in the morning.'

'You're the ward Santa this year?'

'It'll be my fifth time. It's become a tradition.'

The image stayed with Gemma as she returned to the children's room and settled herself in the armchair in the hope of catching at least a little sleep. She could picture Andy in the dayroom. Beside that Christmas tree. Handing out gifts to the small patients he spent his life caring for.

Five times? That meant the first time he'd played the role would have been the year that she'd walked out. He'd never mentioned that he was going to do it.

Why? Because he'd known that she wouldn't understand how he was even able to think of doing it?

How hard would it have been for him that first time? Even on its own, it would have been heartbreaking for a father who'd lost his own son but that year he would have still been reeling from going home to find an empty house the night before.

She'd tried to write Andy a note before she'd left but words had failed her. In the end, the scrap of tearstained paper had held only four words.

'I'm sorry. For everything.'

She'd left it on top of the desk. With her vision blurred by tears she had picked up the nearest available object to attract attention to the piece of paper in the centre of a bare desktop. And the way she'd been feeling, it had seemed appropriate to use that piece of plastic mistletoe.

Gemma heard a snuffle from one of the children and echoed it softly herself. Sleep was not going to release her any time soon, she realised. Her mind was too full. Of memories. Of Andy. Of that kiss on the rooftop with the lights of Santa's sleigh scribing slow circuits in the sky above them.

Her love for Andy hadn't diminished one little bit. Had she done the right thing by setting him free? If he hadn't moved on and found someone else to be the mother of his children, surely the answer was no. And, if the answer *was* no, did that mean there was still a chance for her to be with him?

The way he'd kissed her. Where would that kiss have gone if they hadn't been on a hospital roof in freezing weather?

A smile was competing with the threat of tears now. Gemma knew exactly where that kiss would have gone.

Other emotions were colliding inside her. Echoes of grief that had to come from those shared memories of Max. Guilt at the way she had been so self-obsessed with that grief. Had she really thought that her way of coping had been the right way? That Andy had found it all so much easier?

Sitting here in the dark, surrounded by sleeping children, Gemma was at last in a space where she could see a much bigger picture. It wasn't simply that there were more important things in life than a brilliant career. It was a combination of wisdom gained from isolation. From the devastating loss of a sister she had only stayed in touch with via phone and email for years. From having to step up to become a mother for her nieces and nephews.

Running away and burying herself in her career had been a successful device in hiding from the pain of losing Max but it was only now that she could see the full extent of the collateral damage.

She'd lost the place she thought of as her home.

She'd lost her family. Watching the precious early years of these children growing up.

She'd lost Andy.

Love. That's what she'd taken out of her life.

People and places that she loved and people that she could be loved by.

Emotional safety was a very lonely place.

So lonely that a tiny whimper from Sophie had Gemma on her feet almost eagerly. She laid a gentle hand on the baby's forehead. Her temperature had obviously dropped and her skin felt soft and dry and healthy. Sophie stirred, bringing a small fist up to her mouth. The vigorous sucking noises made Gemma smile.

'You're getting ready to be hungry, darling, aren't you?' she whispered. Reaching into the bassinette, she picked up the bundle of baby and blanket, tucking it into her arms. 'Come on. We'll tiptoe down to the kitchen and see what we can find.'

The ward was beginning to stir. People arriving early for the day shift were quietly preparing to take over from the weary night staff. Fixing a bottle of formula for Sophie, Gemma was greeted by one of the day staff. A nurse called Carla.

'You'll stay for the Christmas breakfast, won't

you?' she asked. 'The night nurses have labelled some spare gifts for the children.'

Could she stay and watch Andy do his thing as Santa? Heaven help her, but she wanted to so much. If she gave in to that desire, though, would it make it that much harder to walk away? It was what she would have to so. Or was it?

That kiss on the roof had done more than awaken too many memories of what being so close to Andy was like. It had planted a seed of hope.

Carla misinterpreted the hesitation she could see on Gemma's face.

'I could get one of the registrars to sign Sophie's discharge form but I'd rather Andy signed you off and...he's going to be a bit busy for a while. He got held up checking our little bone-marrow-transplant girl so he won't have much time to get changed when he gets back. Santa's supposed to make his big entrance at the end of breakfast-time.'

Gemma opened the microwave to rescue the

bottle of warm milk. Sophie reached out for it and whimpered.

'I'll see how we go,' she told Carla. She smiled. 'It's never a quick job getting my lot organised.'

'I'm sure they'd want to stay.' Carla's gaze was frankly curious. 'I hear that Andy's their uncle?'

Gemma's nod was wary. The children didn't know that Andy was still their uncle. On paper, anyway. But of course they'd want to stay.

As much as she did?

Back in the room, Gemma settled into the armchair to feed Sophie, grateful that she still had some time before the other children were likely to wake up. She had to decide what the best thing to do for the children was and she couldn't let that decision be influenced by all the memories and feelings that had been stirred into life for her again. What if the children found out about Andy's relationship to them but he wanted nothing more to do with them? They had suffered the loss of too many adults in their lives already.

The last of the bottle had been hungrily guzzled and Gemma was holding Sophie up against her shoulder to burp her when Hazel woke up. There was enough light in the room for her to see the way her niece's eyes snapped open fully as she registered her unfamiliar surroundings. She heard the sharp, fearful intake of breath.

'It's OK, hon,' she said softly. 'You're safe. Everything's fine.'

Hazel's gasp turned into a sigh of relief as she scrambled into a sitting position.

'I need to wee,' she informed Gemma.

'Can you wait for a sec?' Gemma made faster circles on Sophie's back and patted it a few times. 'Soph will get grumpy if she doesn't have a burp.' She sniffed. 'And I think she's overdue for a nappy change, too, but I can do that after I show you where the bathroom is.'

'I can go to the loo by myself,' Hazel said with some indignation. 'I'm *seven*.'

'I know. I just thought…being in a strange place…'

'I can manage.' But Hazel hesitated when she got to the door. 'Which way do I go?'

'Left.' Gemma tilted her head for emphasis because both her hands were full of baby. 'If you can't see a door that has a sign saying "Bathroom", just go a bit further and you'll find a nurse you can ask. They're all very nice.'

Hazel nodded, went outside the door and looked up and down the corridor. She couldn't see anybody in either direction.

Which way was left again?

Andy eyed the big, plastic rubbish sack on the chair. He needed to go and find a spare pillow or two to stuff under the red jacket of the Santa suit the sack contained. And was that special glue still in the smaller bag containing the fake beard? It had taken some time to find that glue again. Why on earth had he put it in his desk drawer?

Andy opened the sack, lifting out the red hat with white trim on the top to have a look but then he paused, hat in hand, turning his head very slowly. An odd prickle on the back of his neck suggested he wasn't alone.

Glancing over his shoulder, he found his instincts hadn't deceived him. A small girl was standing, framed by the office doorway. She was wearing hospital-issue pyjamas but she wasn't a patient.

'Hazel.' A beat of alarm pulsed through Andy. Had Gemma sent her oldest niece to find him? Why couldn't she come herself? 'What's up, chicken?'

Hazel's bottom lip quivered. 'I went to find the loo,' she said, 'and…I got lost.'

'Oh, no…' Andy's smile was sympathetic. He dropped the hat he was still holding onto the top of the bag and held his hand out towards Hazel. He could fix this. He could show her where the toilet was.

But, with a sob, Hazel launched herself at him and Andy found himself scooping the small girl into his arms to give her a cuddle.

'Hey…it's not that bad. You didn't really get lost cos you found me.'

'That's not why I'm crying,' Hazel sobbed.

'What is it, then?' Andy wasn't used to holding distressed children. He might be in the same room but there were always parents or nurses to do the cuddling. He'd almost forgotten what it was like to have small arms entwined around his neck as though he was some kind of giant lifesaver.

'It's…' Hazel unfurled one arm to point at the Santa hat that had slid from the top of the sack to land on the floor. 'It's *Christmas*.'

Andy nodded. 'So it is. But…it's supposed to be a happy day, you know.'

'Not…not when you don't have a mummy or daddy any more.'

'No.' Andy closed his eyes for a moment and held Hazel closer. This was the first Christmas for these children since they had become orphans. As the oldest, Hazel would have the clearest memories of their parents and she would be missing them most. 'I'm sorry about that, chicken. It's really sad, isn't it?'

'Mmm.' Hazel snuffled and then sniffed loudly.

'Would you like a tissue?'

'No…' She ducked her head and wiped her nose on her pyjama sleeve. 'S'okay.'

'But you'd like to go to the toilet?'

'Yes.'

'Come on, then.' Andy put her down. Hazel's fingers caught on his name badge as he lowered her to the floor. Then she took his hand and let him lead her out into the corridor and down towards the bathroom.

'My last name is Gillespie,' she told him.

'I know.'

'Your name's on your badge.'

'It is.'

'Why have you got the same name as Aunty Gemma?'

'Because...' Oh, help. Andy's respect for children meant that he always tried to be as honest as he could within the limits of their understanding. How much did Hazel know? Or remember? 'Gemma's got the same name as me because we got married.'

'When?'

'A long time ago. Before you were born even. Here's the bathroom. I'll wait out here for you and make sure you don't get lost going back to your room.'

Hazel was back in a commendably short time. She slipped her hand into Andy's without hesitation and the trusting gesture was heart-melting.

'Gemma's Mummy's sister,' she told Andy.

'I know.'

'Are you mummy's brother, then?'

'Kind of. I married your mummy's sister so that made me something called a brother-in-law to your mummy.'

Hazel looked confused.

'I'm...I was your uncle,' he added.

Hazel looked even more confused. 'Why did you stop being my uncle?'

'I...didn't.' Whatever had melted inside him moments before had congealed into something hard now. He'd missed these children far more than he'd realised. They had been part of his family. The closest thing he'd had to children of his own after losing Max.

'So I can still call you "Uncle"?'

'Sure.'

Hazel tried it out. 'Uncle...Andy...'

Could she remember using the name? He could

remember. He could actually hear an echo of a three-year-old's gleeful shriek as he came through the front door of that wonderful old, converted barn.

'If you're still our uncle, how come you never come to visit us, then?'

A fair question but he couldn't tell a seven-year-old it was because it had been simply too painful. That the children were part of Gemma and if she didn't want him in her life any more, he'd felt that maybe he had no right to keep any part of her family.

'I don't know, chicken. I'm sorry. I should have.'

If he'd kept up contact with Gemma's family, he would have known about the tragedy. He could have been there for Gemma. He might have been able to re-establish contact with her and not have had to live with the awful silence of the last four years. But that was exactly why he'd let the contact lapse in the first place.

It had been Gemma's choice to leave and she'd ignored his attempts to track her down by phone. She hadn't wanted to live with him any more. Not even in the same country. She hadn't wanted to talk to him. She'd wanted space and he'd given it to her. And the weeks had turned into months and he had kept putting off making contact that would probably deal another blow of rejection. And then the months had turned into years. How on earth had he let that happen?

'So why did you stop being married to Aunty Gemma?' Hazel asked as they neared the door to her room.

Tricky question. How could Andy answer that without getting into a complicated discussion about divorce laws?

'We haven't stopped being married, exactly,' he said awkwardly. 'We just haven't been living together.'

'Why not? Aunty Gemma's nice.' Hazel stopped outside the door to their room and gave Andy a very steady glance. 'Aunty Gemma's our mummy now.'

'I know. You're very lucky. She *is* nice.'

Hazel opened the door. Jamie was getting dressed. The twins were standing up in the cot, blinking sleepily. Chloe had her thumb in her mouth. Ben was holding Digger under his arm.

Gemma was changing Sophie's nappy. 'You've been gone a long time, hon,' she said, without looking up. 'I was getting worried.' Sticking the last piece of tape into place, she looked up to see Andy standing beside Hazel and she stilled.

'Oh…hi…'

'Hey…' Andy responded.

They both seemed to be at a complete loss for words. Standing there staring at each other like embarrassed teenagers on a first date. Was Gemma's head suddenly filled with that kiss? Like his was?

Hazel looked at Gemma and then at Andy. Then at Gemma again.

'Uncle Andy says you're still married.'

'O…' Gemma bit her lip. 'That's…true, I guess.'

'And you're our mummy now.'

'Also true.'

Hazel nodded as though she had finally sorted out something important in her mind. She turned back and looked up at Andy.

'That means you're our daddy now, doesn't it?'
Oh…no…

Gemma saw the way the colour drained out of Andy's face. He looked around at all the children in the room and then opened his mouth to say something but didn't get the chance because a nurse appeared beside him.

'I just came to see if you guys needed a hand with anything in here,' the nurse said cheerfully.

Andy muttered something completely unintelligible, stepped back, turned and strode away.

Gemma could feel every step of his increasing the distance between them and something finally snapped. She couldn't let him walk out like this. Not after the bombshell that Hazel had just dropped.

'Yes,' she told the nurse. She handed Sophie over. 'Please watch the children for a few minutes. I have to…'

She didn't know quite *what* she had to do.

She just knew she had to do *something* and it could possibly be the most important thing she was ever going to do in her life.

Right at this moment, it felt like her life depended on it.

Her sentence didn't need to be finished in any case because she was already outside the room. She could see Andy at some distance down the corridor. Already past where his office was. Where was he going?

Gemma started running.

'Andy….*wait for me…*'

CHAPTER ELEVEN

ANDY was heading for the stairs.

An escape route. To the roof, maybe, for some more fresh air?

He heard the sound of Gemma's voice behind him.

'Andy....*please* wait.'

No. Not the roof. Not when the last time he'd been there was still so fresh in his memory. He could feel that kiss, all over again, in every cell of his body.

He could feel the desire.

And the confusion.

The wanting to open himself up to Gemma again.

The fear that came with knowing how much pain that could cause. Was he strong enough to go through that again? Did he want to even go there?

He didn't really have a choice. Not when he could sense the speed and urgency with which Gemma was approaching him. When he could hear the desperate plea in her voice.

Andy stopped and turned to face Gemma.

She almost skidded to a halt just a few feet away from him. She must have run all the way from the children's room because she needed to catch her breath for a moment. At least it gave Andy the chance to say something first, instead of waiting for the axe to fall.

'I'm sorry,' he said. 'I shouldn't have said anything to Hazel. But she noticed that our names were still the same. We *are* still married…legally, anyway…and…I like to be honest with kids if I can be.'

Gemma nodded. She opened her mouth and then closed it again. She took in a great gulp of air.

'Why?' The word came out in a kind of croak.

Andy raised his eyebrows. 'Don't you think it's a good thing to be honest?'

Gemma shook her head with a sharp movement. 'No…*why* are we still married?'

Here it came, Andy thought. The axe. There was no reason for them to still be married so Gemma was about to ask him to set divorce proceedings in place.

Her eyes were searching his face. 'I've been waiting to hear from you. I thought you would have found someone else long before this. Someone who could give you the baby you wanted. Someone who…who could make you happy.'

Her voice broke.

Andy stared at her. Behind them, kitchen staff were pushing the breakfast trolleys into the ward and the smell of bacon and eggs and other breakfast treats filled the air. The trolleys had strings of bells attached to them and the kitchen staff were singing 'Jingle Bells' with great enthusiasm for so early in the morning.

Andy barely heard them and was only vaguely aware of the smell of hot food. His focus was on Gemma. On what she was saying, of course, but more the look on her face.

'Was that really what you thought would happen when you left?'

Gemma nodded. She had a tear rolling down the side of her nose. 'You wanted to start again. You wanted a Christmas tree and…and you wanted a baby. I couldn't give you anything you wanted but…I wanted you to be happy because… because I love you so much.'

Love?

Not *loved*?

Andy shook his head. He let his breath out in a huff that was almost laughter. 'How the hell did you expect me to be *happy* when I didn't have you?'

'Because…you weren't happy with me.'

The statement was so simple.

But so huge.

'I'm sorry.' The words came from somewhere very deep inside Andy. A space he had tried to stay away from for a very long time. 'I've wanted to say it a million times but I thought it was far too late.'

'What are *you* sorry for? It's me that messed things up in the end.'

'I'm sorry I couldn't help you. I knew you were hurting but there seemed to be nothing I could do that would help. In the end, I guess I gave up trying.'

'You were hurting just as much. *I'm* sorry.' Gemma sniffed and rubbed at her nose. 'I know I made it harder for you…'

'I think we made it harder for each other, even if it was the last thing we wanted to do.'

'But you tried to help me. I just made your life hell. You *said* that.'

He had. He couldn't deny it. The echo was right there.

'It's been two years of hell…'

'I'm sorry. I—'

'I couldn't understand,' Gemma cut in, 'the way you were dealing with it all. I couldn't see what you got out of being near other children. Maybe I never would have if I hadn't been thrown into being a mother figure.'

Andy felt his lips twist at the irony of the cards

fate had chosen to deal. 'It was the last thing you ever wanted to be, wasn't it? A stay-at-home mum to a big bunch of kids?'

Gemma's voice was soft. 'Losing someone as precious as a person is a very fast way of learning what's really important in life. I should have learned that way back when we lost Max. Maybe I would have if I hadn't been so completely numb for so long.'

'I'm so sorry you had to learn it the way you did. Laura was very special.'

Gemma's nod was jerky. 'She was. But she's not the only person I love that I lost.'

'No. Evan was great, too.'

'I wasn't talking about Ev either.'

The way Gemma was looking at him was... heart-breaking. He'd never seen her looking so forlorn. So vulnerable.

And then it hit him.

She was talking about *him*.

Andy could feel that glow again. The one he'd felt when he'd gone into the reception area in the emergency department and seen her again for the first time in so long. Shafts of it were coming from beneath the lid he'd slammed over the hole it lived in. If he let it out, was it possible that the light would be bright enough to blind him to the pain?

Was it really true that she'd left him because she wanted him to be happy? And she thought he'd be happier *without* her?

How stupid was that?

If Gemma kept looking at him like that, the glow couldn't do anything but get stronger. It was so strong already that it was pushing up that lid without any conscious effort on his part.

Andy took a deep, deep breath.

'You haven't lost me, Gem,' he said quietly.

'You haven't found someone else?'

'I tried,' Andy admitted. He gave his head a small, sad shake. 'But they weren't you.'

Somehow, without either of them taking a noticeable step, they had come closer together. Within touching distance but only their eyes were holding each other's.

'I can't ask you to take on a ready-made family.' Gemma's smile wobbled. 'I've got five kids. *Five.*'

'They're already part of my family,' Andy said. 'They always have been. I've just been…absent from *their* lives.'

'You and me both.'

'You've made up for it now.'

'I'm trying. But I don't want to put any pressure on you. We don't have to rush anything, Andy.' Gemma's smile was still wobbling. 'It's enough to know that you don't hate me. That… there might still be a chance…'

'Hate you? As if I could.' Andy was watching her lips. They'd been trembling like that up on the roof, hadn't they? He'd cured that by kissing her.

He could do it again.

He moved closer.

'Andy?' The call was urgent. 'Thank goodness…I've found you.' Carla sounded anxious. 'Breakfast is nearly finished. Why aren't you in the Santa suit?'

* * *

The dayroom was packed as full as a can of sardines.

Beds lined the walls for the children who weren't mobile. There were wheelchairs tucked into corners, adults holding small children in their arms and a group of children, nurses and parents sitting cross-legged on the floor.

Christmas music was playing, the lights on the Christmas tree were sparkling and Santa was sitting in all his red and white glory on a throne that looked suspiciously like an adult-sized wheelchair covered by an old red velvet curtain.

Gemma was standing just inside the door. She had Sophie in her arms, who was sleeping like a little angel. Hazel was pressed to one side and she had a twin clutching each of her legs. Jamie had edged closer to the children sitting on the carpet. Gemma was very proud of how well her little family was behaving. And she was selfishly delighted as well because it gave her the chance to simply stand there and enjoy looking at Andy.

She was loving seeing how much pleasure he

was getting playing his part in giving so many children a happy day. And every so often, when he was waiting for a new parcel to appear from the sack or another child to come and share centre stage, his gaze would stray toward the door.

To where Gemma was standing.

As if he wanted to reassure himself that she was still here.

That he hadn't imagined the urgent, whispered exchange of plans for the rest of today as Carla had supervised his attention to important Christmas duties.

He would go home with Gemma and the children after he was finished here. They could all have some time together. All of them.

And later, when the children were in bed, they would be able to talk.

Really talk.

The way they had all those years ago? Before they had carried such a burden of grief? Before they had been tired and stressed new parents even?

The way they had when they had been starting

out perhaps. So very much in love, with a future in which almost anything had seemed possible.

They were both older and wiser now.

If they still loved each other enough, surely anything *was* possible.

Every time Andy's gaze found hers, Gemma found herself feeling more and more hopeful.

The touch of eye contact was like a physical caress that became steadily easier. More familiar. Touching a little deeper every time. Trusting a little more every time. How crazy was it that they could be so far apart in a crowded room and be getting closer with every passing minute?

It was magic.

Christmas magic.

'Ho, ho, ho,' Santa boomed. 'Do I have another present in my sack?'

A young nurse wearing a very cute elf costume reached into the sack and produced both a parcel and a very wide smile.

'It's for John Boy,' she announced.

Santa peered over his gold-rimmed spectacles. 'Is there a John Boy here?'

'It's *me*.' John Boy looked around the whole room to make sure everybody had heard the exciting news and his smile was enough to create a ripple of laughter.

The parcel for John Boy was the largest one yet and he couldn't wait to rip the wrapping paper off.

'It's a box of magic tricks,' he said in awe.

'Better than jokes.' Santa nodded. 'You won't find any plastic vomit in there, lad.'

John Boy grinned. 'How do you know about that?'

Santa wasn't disconcerted in the least. The fluffy beard moved as he grinned and he tapped the side of his nose with a white-gloved hand. The lights on the tree made his spectacles shine as he looked up. Gemma was close enough to see the crinkles at the corners of his eyes as he smiled at her.

He'd been about to kiss her before, when Carla had interrupted them, but it didn't matter. There would be plenty of time for that later.

Nothing needed to be rushed.

As corny as she knew it was to even think it, Gemma couldn't help reminding herself that today was the first day of the rest of her life.

Of their lives.

And it was Christmas. Having Andy back in her life would be the most priceless gift she could ever receive.

Her eyes were misty as she led the twins up to receive the gifts Santa's elf had found near the bottom of the sack with their names on.

How priceless a gift would it be to these children if they could have Andy as a father?

The sack seemed to be bottomless.

Gift after gift had been distributed. There was a sea of wrapping paper on the floor. His elf had trotted back and forth to give parcels to the children in their beds and she'd even put on a special elf mask to give Ruthie her present on the other side of the glass windows where she was standing with her parents to watch. The extras in attendance, like siblings of patients and all the

Gillespie children, had been given small presents to let them feel included.

Surely, surely it was almost over.

He could take off this astonishingly hot outfit and he could leave work. He could go with Gemma and the children and find the time and space they needed to…to put things right?

To start again?

Andy had no idea what the immediate future held. What he did know was that he was feeling more alive than he had done for years. Bursting with it, in fact. He couldn't wait to step into that future.

Because Gemma would be there.

And the children.

His family.

The elf produced yet another parcel. It looked like a late entry. The size and shape suggested a very generic bar of chocolate.

'It's for Gemma.' Even the elf was losing a little of her enthusiasm.

John Boy hadn't pushed his wheelchair very far away after receiving his gift. He was inspecting a black bag and a plastic egg that were clearly the components of a magic trick but he looked up at the announcement.

'Who's Gemma?'

Carla had taken Sophie, and Gemma was picking her way towards him through the crowd, looking embarrassed at being included.

Andy smiled. 'Gemma's...'

What could he say? There were more people than John Boy who seemed to be interested in his response. Carla's eyebrows were very high. His elf had her mouth open.

Who was Gemma indeed? Could he call her his wife? No. It was too soon. It would be making assumptions that he had no right to make no matter how much he might want to believe in them.

But then his gaze caught Gemma's as she came closer.

And he knew. He just knew that everything was going to be all right. He could see a reflection of love that was every bit as strong as the love he was feeling for her.

'Gemma's my wife,' he told John Boy.

It felt *so* good to say that.

So right.

Gemma seemed to think so, too, because she was smiling. And crying? She certainly wasn't looking where she was going, which was probably why she tripped on the footplate of John Boy's wheelchair.

Andy leapt off the Christmas throne to catch her before she fell.

John Boy was grinning from ear to ear.

'That makes her Mrs Santa,' he said loudly.

The world seemed to stop spinning for a moment. Was it really all right for this to be happening so fast? So publicly?

'Hmm...' Andy needed to let Gemma know she wasn't under pressure here. 'I guess it might.'

Gemma was laughing.

'I think it does,' she said.

Andy caught his breath. 'Do you want to be Mrs Santa?'

She was looking up at him, those amazing eyes dancing with joy. 'If you're Santa, then yes...of course I want to be Mrs Santa.'

'That's good.' Andy finally remembered to use his Santa voice again. 'Because I have a present for you.'

'It's chocolate,' John Boy said.

'Maybe I have another present for Gemma,' Santa said.

'What is it?'

The question came from John Boy but when Andy hesitated he could suddenly feel way too many pairs of eyes on him.

'Where is it?' John Boy demanded.

'In my pocket,' Andy admitted. He was talking to Gemma now. Only Gemma. He dropped his voice to a whisper that none of the children could overhear. 'I found it in the desk drawer this morning when I was looking for the beard glue.'

Gemma knew what it was.

He'd kept it? After all these years?

That scrappy little piece of plastic mistletoe?

Yes. There it was. He was holding it above her head.

And Santa was kissing her. Amongst the tickle of all that white fluff, she could feel the warmth of Andy's lips. The strength of his love.

The promise of the future.

'Eww.' John Boy was joyously disgusted by the display.

But everyone else seemed to think it was a bonus gift. Gemma could hear clapping. Cheers even.

Nothing to compare with what she could see in Andy's eyes, though.

The joy.

The hope.

'Let's go home,' Andy said softly. 'I have a sleigh that's not far away.'

Gemma held his gaze. 'Does it have room for a few kids?'

'It was made for kids. And you. Especially you.'

'*Oi...*' John Boy's voice was stern. 'You're not going to start that kissing stuff again, are you?'

Gemma and Andy looked at each other. And smiled.

Of course they were. But not yet. Not here.

'Yes, please, Santa,' Gemma whispered. 'Let's go home.'

* * * * *

Mills & Boon® Large Print
Medical

June

July

August

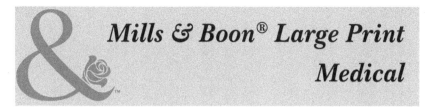

Mills & Boon® Large Print Medical

September

NYC ANGELS: REDEEMING THE PLAYBOY   Carol Marinelli
NYC ANGELS: HEIRESS'S BABY SCANDAL   Janice Lynn
ST PIRAN'S: THE WEDDING!   Alison Roberts
SYDNEY HARBOUR HOSPITAL: EVIE'S BOMBSHELL   Amy Andrews
THE PRINCE WHO CHARMED HER   Fiona McArthur
HIS HIDDEN AMERICAN BEAUTY   Connie Cox

October

NYC ANGELS: UNMASKING DR SERIOUS   Laura Iding
NYC ANGELS: THE WALLFLOWER'S SECRET   Susan Carlisle
CINDERELLA OF HARLEY STREET   Anne Fraser
YOU, ME AND A FAMILY   Sue MacKay
THEIR MOST FORBIDDEN FLING   Melanie Milburne
THE LAST DOCTOR SHE SHOULD EVER DATE   Louisa George

November

NYC ANGELS: FLIRTING WITH DANGER   Tina Beckett
NYC ANGELS: TEMPTING NURSE SCARLET   Wendy S. Marcus
ONE LIFE CHANGING MOMENT   Lucy Clark
P.S. YOU'RE A DADDY!   Dianne Drake
RETURN OF THE REBEL DOCTOR   Joanna Neil
ONE BABY STEP AT A TIME   Meredith Webber

0513 LP 2P P2 Medical